Cottonmouth

Eric A. Yancy, MD

Published in the United States.

ISBN: 978-1-09838-914-7 (paperback)
ISBN: 978-1-09838-915-4 (ebook)

Editing by Stephanie McGuire
Proofreading by Rachel Stevens
Cover and Text Design by Kathleen Dyson
Cover images © iStockphoto.com: "Cottonmouth Snake"by negaprion; "DNA" by ktsimage; "COVID-19" by Jongho Shin.

*This book is dedicated to the hundreds of thousands
of our loved ones who have lost their lives to
COVID 19, and the brave citizens of our society who
fought in every way to protect them.*

1

"I'LL TAKE BIOCHEMISTRY FOR 1000, ALEX."

"It's an organometallic chemical reaction in which alkyl, allyl, vinyl or aryl-magnesium halides add to a carbonyl group in an aldehyde or ketone."

"What is a Grignard reaction?" the aging, retired professor muttered.

"What is the Grignard reaction?" the young contestant answered.

"Hah! I got another one," Professor Alton McGuire exclaimed to his barely awake wife. It had become a nightly ritual since the pandemic lockdown. He would sit and watch all of the old shows on the classic TV channel, except for Jeopardy, which aired on a different channel, and she would sit dutifully on the couch pretending to be interested.

"I could have been on that show, but the arthritis in my fingers would never let me push the signaler fast enough," the elderly professor playfully lamented.

"Yes, Al, I'm sure you could have."

They were both right. In his earlier years Alton McGuire had been nothing short of a genius. As a member of the molecular biology department, he had been the youngest recipient of a full professorship in the history of Richards College. His students were fascinated by his ability to teach very challenging subject matter while he kept them laughing at the same time. His anecdotes about growing up on a farm in rural Louisiana were legendary. Toward the end of his career, he had chosen to return to his home state and retire there.

The professor's barely perceptible limp was a testament to his former life. Once a promising athlete, his career had been cut short by a tractor incident. One scorching Louisiana morning he had taken the tractor to till the small strip of land his family owned. A small calf broke away from its mother and darted directly in front of the tractor. In a valiant effort to avoid the young renegade, Al whipped the tractor sharply to the right, missing the calf by inches. Unfortunately, he was moving with such speed that the tractor's center of gravity shifted just enough to flip him over. He tried to dive from the seat, but the huge left wheel of the tractor snapped his ankle and came to rest on it. Trapped underneath, Al cried out as searing, blistering pain throbbed up and down his entire leg. Two workers, having seen the accident, raced to free him.

He was rushed to the general hospital in the back of his father's old pickup truck. He could still remember the signs with the arrows. The anguished crew took him to the door marked "COLORED" and waited. Eventually an old doctor showed up and unceremoniously snapped the bone into position. Decades later the professor still remembered the sound and the pain associated with the realignment process. Although the gray-haired practitioner had felt sympathy toward his athletic patient, he also realized early on that the leg would never be the same. With limited time to spend on a young colored boy, he hastily but compassionately gave instructions to Al's parents and then retreated into the bustle of the emergency room.

The leg took weeks to heal, as the fracture extended through the growth plate. Years later in his anatomy class, Al would learn that, according to the most recent medical advances, his injury would have been classified as a type IV Salter-Harris fracture. That kind of fracture absolutely required an operation by a skilled orthopedic surgeon. But in rural Louisiana in the 1950s? No such luck. Even if there had been a surgeon available, the care on the "COLORED" ward would not have allowed for such luxuries.

Al's high school team was devastated. There were no speed radar guns back then, but every coach Al encountered, including the ones he played against, said they had never seen a young pitcher throw that hard. They liked to say that he would have given Don Newcombe a run for his money. In his short career, Al had already thrown three no-hitters. His fastball was virtually unhittable. With very little form or windup, he would just rear back and let it fly.

By that point, Al had already been a disciple of baseball for a long time. As a small boy he had loved listening to the old AM radio that broadcast the closest team to his town, the St. Louis Cardinals. The radio would only come in late at night, so he usually couldn't hear the games until nearly midnight. He would take the little hand-held radio and listen to the West Coast teams' night games because that was the only time slot compatible with his finicky AM receiver. By the time he was in high school, Al's strategic insight into baseball was as outsized as his physical gifts.

But the accident irreversibly affected his balance. Al could never again plant and throw straight. Underneath the wheels of a used and patched together John Deere tractor, his Hall of Fame career had ended before it had really begun. Al tried other positions, but pitching was his first and only love. The loss of his athletic career led Al into a deep depression. One night, a few days after his final baseball practice, he tried staying up late to listen to the sports radio broadcast he had always loved. After only a few seconds of hearing the night game announcers, he hurled the hand-held radio across his bedroom, hot tears traveling down to the corners of his mouth.

During the weeks and months he was unable to work in the field, or to do the barn chores, Al would drag his extremely heavy, and filthy, plaster of Paris cast down to the watering pond. He would sit under the old Chinaberry tree. Its leaves were small, and it didn't give much shade, but at least it was a little out of the sun. Al watched nature. He watched where grass grew and where it didn't. He watched the paths of the ants and the larvae that ate the leaves. He was fascinated by these observations, but his mind wanted to go so much deeper. Tentatively, Al began to visit the school library. Weekly visits turned into daily pilgrimages, and, sitting against the shelves day after day, Al devoured books about plant and animal life. He peppered all of his science teachers with urgent, burning questions. Knowing *what* was happening was interesting, but knowing *why* it was happening amazed him. Out of the depression caused by losing the sport he desperately loved, Al's true calling began to slowly take shape.

There was little doubt what path he would take after graduation. The valedictorian of G.W. Carver High School was destined to become a scientist. Al felt compelled to study the mysteries of biology and discover why things were as they were.

Marnie shifted on the couch and asked, "What's for dinner Sunday?"

"Shhh!!!" Al furiously whispered. "It's the Final Jeopardy category, and I need to figure out how much to bet."

"The final Jeopardy category today is sixteenth-century monarchs," the host said.

Al burst into laughter and blurted out, "I will bet twenty-five cents Alex!"

Marnie snickered right along with Al before gently repeating, "I said what do you want for dinner Sunday?"

This question usually brought on their customary three back-and-forths of "I don't care, what do you want?" but on this particular day Al actually answered.

"You know, Marnie," he said quietly, "I would love to have one of your sweet potato casseroles."

"Fair enough," Marnie agreed. "No problem at all."

Later Al would come to realize how one simple answer to one simple question had altered his life forever.

2

AT SEVENTY-FIVE YEARS OLD, MARNIE WAS STILL STUNNING.
"Who says mature ladies can't be hotties?" Al would muse every so often.
Each time, Marnie would answer in exactly the same way. "Oh go away,"
she would tease, "You are prejudiced!" But she enjoyed her husband's com-
pliment. Marigold Nelda Jackson had indeed been a looker. In contrast
to Al, she'd been raised in the city—if you can call downtown Jackson,
Mississippi in the 1950s the city. The two-sport athlete, cheerleader, and
very first female student council president had been the talk of the school.
She had missed being valedictorian of her senior class by mere percentage
points and somehow never forgot it. For the rest of her life, Marnie carried
a determination to make up for that perceived failure.

Marnie's passion was education. She loved teaching little ones and
would often say with a warm twinkle, "First through fifth are my grades.
By sixth grade they are way too grown and think they know it all!"
She worked in the public school system until her retirement, and her
reputation as a skilled educator preceded her. On a yearly basis, prestigious offers from several of the most prominent private schools would
reach Marnie's desk. Every year she would carefully craft a gracious letter
declining each offer. She knew she was among the best in the country

at what she did and always felt that her efforts, no, her *calling*, was with children who started out with so much less than others.

Each Mother's Day, Al and Marnie's mailbox was full of cards from former students—CEOs, doctors, nurses, teachers, school principals, and successful members of dozens of other professions. They all wanted to thank Mrs. McGuire for everything she had done for them in school.

───────

Al and Marnie met in a strange way, in a meeting that felt awkward to both of them. During graduate school, Al worked as a teaching assistant for freshman biology. Marnie was still a senior, only one year behind Al, so she should have never been in his class. But she had thrown herself into student teaching and committed so much time to volunteering that she missed taking one freshman-level class she needed to graduate. That is how Marnie—with only a passing interest in science—ended up in Biology 101. She scanned the student catalog, chose the least of the available evils, and grabbed up the last computer punch card.

Marnie knew that she would be able to pass biology just by showing up, but she wanted to make sure she at least appeared to be interested on the first day. The young TA with the almost imperceptible limp entered and proceeded to take roll call. Marnie never quite figured out why, but she felt the subtle flutter of butterflies in her belly whenever she looked at the young man with piercing intelligence behind his eyes. She quickly suppressed the feeling and put it out of her mind. The teaching assistant called the roll in a mundane manner until he came to one name.

"Marigold Jackson," he said and looked around. He tried desperately to hide his reaction but *Marigold*?! Who names a child Marigold? Al never figured out how, but his internal chuckling must have momentarily shown itself on his face. He brilliantly recovered, or so he thought, by feigning a cough to try and cover up his glee.

The keen eyes that would later see Billy pass a note to Johnny in the fifth row were not fooled. These were the eyes that would catch a fight brewing three hundred yards away on the school playground or detect the slight eye twitch of a student betraying the lie they had just uttered.

Marnie hung out for a couple of minutes after class, slowly packing up her notebooks and class syllabus. As the last freshman walked out of the door, she approached the TA's desk.

"Do you find my name funny?"

"Excuse me?" the stunned young man said.

"Do you find my name funny?" Marigold asked again.

"I'm sorry but I don't know your name."

"I thought maybe you found my name funny because you laughed when you called the roll. Is this the type of instruction I can expect from a so-called teaching assistant? Am I to expect the same type of sophomoric discourse I hear from the fifth graders whom I student teach?"

A very thin line of sweat now started to creep its way into the hairline of Al's three-inch afro. This very attractive young woman, obviously not a freshman, was now calling him out for an offense he had done his best to conceal and barely remembered committing.

"I am so sorry Miss …"

"Marigold Jackson," she all but spat at him.

As Al would later fondly recall, there must have been the slightest twitch of the zygomaticus major muscle in his face causing a split-second micro-smile, but Marigold Jackson caught it.

"You are *still* at it?"

"No, no, Miss Jackson, my face just twitches like that. I think it's the caffeine."

"Have you ever heard of decaf? Maybe you should switch types."

With that, Marigold turned and walked away, leaving Al mesmerized by her unusual combination of backbone and free-spiritedness.

For the rest of the semester, Biology 101 felt like a high-wire act for Al. Each time a question was raised and Marigold's hand went up, he was ever so careful to say, "Miss Jackson?" She seemed to enjoy his discomfort. In fact, Marnie was delighted that torturing the TA was actually helping her ace the class. She had to know all of the answers if she wanted to watch him squirm. Twelve weeks later when handing back the final examination blue books, Al called each student by their first and last names. But when he reached the exam with a bright red "100%" on the cover, he merely said, "Miss Jackson" and handed her the blue book, his dark eyes sparkling.

As class dismissed that day, Marnie was essentially a graduate. There was nothing left for her but the commencement ceremony; Al knew his window was closing. On her way out of the room, once again the last to exit, she heard the TA's soft voice behind her.

"Decaf?"

Marnie turned and looked at the junior professor to be. "Where?" was her only reply.

Al's face broke into the widest grin as he said, "Faculty coffee shop? I can get you in now. I have connections."

Decades later Marnie could still spark that wide grin whenever she wanted to. If ever she and Al had a serious argument, and there were very few, she would simply turn her head, walk away and say, "Decaf." Game, set, match.

3

AFTER THEIR FIRST DATE AT THE FACULTY COFFEE SHOP, Al and Marnie went on an uneventful second date at the movies. Catching a double feature together proved to be a pleasant way to spend the evening, and inevitably led to Al's request for a dinner date. Since both Al and Marnie were pursuing graduate degrees, money was in short supply. Despite that fact, Al was determined to give his new interest an impressive evening. He knew of a quaint restaurant nestled in a small village a few miles out of town. Al had passed and seen it on a number of occasions, and from the outside it looked like a romantic spot. True to its Southern theme, the restaurant was built in the style of a boat.

When Al arrived to pick Marnie up from the family home where she was renting a small room, she looked stunning. A serious student more concerned with academics than fashion, she wore a stylish knit sweater dress that gently accented her curves. "Um, wow," Al thought. If she had gotten a little dressed up like this maybe her interest was parallel with his? Ever the gentleman, Al opened the door, and Marnie stepped inside his ancient Chevy. There were only two clean places in the vehicle. Al occupied one, and his date now occupied the other. Al had taken great pains to wash the car, but there were still traces of a busy graduate student's life all over the back seat. They drove to the restaurant and stepped inside. Its entire theme was crafted around a luxurious yacht.

Al's first hint that there was a problem should have been the question from the hostess.

"Do you have a reservation?"

It had not occurred to him to make a reservation because most of the places he ate did not require one. The hostess assured him it would not be a problem, and to Al's relief he and Marnie were seated.

Trying not to stare at his date, Al missed the second clue regarding the caliber of his dining choice: leather-bound menus. Marnie took hers, and the server graciously poured water and left a full basket of bread on the table in front of them. Al was aware he was racking up many points now in the impression category. Never a real fan of seafood, odd considering his Louisiana roots, Al turned to the steak section. Marnie perused the menu and looked over the top of it, giving her date a slight smile. He found what he was looking for. One ribeye steak. As he read the preparation guide—*rare, medium rare, medium, medium well, well done*—his eyes drifted to the right. In the far-right margin were the prices.

When he saw them, three things rose simultaneously: his heart rate, his respiratory rate and his blood pressure. Instinctively, Al realized he was experiencing the three signs of catecholamine-induced panic. His fight or flight response had just kicked in. Since there was nothing to fight, it appeared flight was the next best option. He found himself in quite the dilemma. Here he was with his date in a mortifying situation because he had just not done his homework. How could one steak cost twenty-five dollars? As he squirmed in his seat, he felt for his wallet. He could not let Marnie see him checking his money, so he excused himself to make a phone call. He told Marnie he had forgotten to reserve one of the labs for his class the next day and needed to call the attendant. Marnie smiled and tried not to giggle. Her date's lie was so ridiculous she could barely suppress her laughter.

Al left the table and made his way to the alcove that held the bank of three pay phones. He reached in his pocket and pulled out all of his cash. Including coins he had $23.52. He searched each pocket twice hoping more cash would magically appear, but none did. Al returned to the table and sat down. Because Marnie had closed her menu, Al was sure she had decided on her dinner entrée, and a small, fist-sized ball of dread formed in his stomach. Then he did something that Marnie admired greatly. He looked her in the eye and said, "I have made a mistake and I am really sorry. I did not check the prices here because I was so excited about bringing you here. There is absolutely nothing on this menu I can afford. We are going to have to leave."

Marnie just smiled and said, "Sure. Let's go."

Al was hooked.

The couple silently left their table, and as they walked from the restaurant toward the car, Al was quiet.

Marnie sensed his embarrassment and, once seated in the car, touched his arm, waited a beat, and said, "I get to choose the restaurant next time."

Next time? Al thought. After this fiasco there would be a next time? He was *really* hooked then. Marigold Jackson was a keeper.

Marnie never let on that she knew Al could not afford the restaurant as soon as they had sat down. The first thing she did when she opened the menu was look at the prices. She hadn't really selected an entrée because she knew they would not be eating there. Instead she imagined a delicious hamburger with crispy fries and a Coke. The guy had been nice and brave enough to admit he had made a mistake. She could easily live with that. Whenever Marnie would tell the story to any of her friends, each would say, "That would have been the last I saw of him." Marnie would just smile and think to herself, "Your loss."

4

IF SENTIENT CHARACTERISTICS COULD BE ASSIGNED TO A virus, the story of strain Q47cx would be easy to tell.

Virus Q47cx's ancestors had been around for hundreds of years, occasionally causing mild illness in humans but largely staying in the subhuman populations. In 2002, renegades of this viral clan decided to try their luck by producing more serious illnesses in humans. There is no good explanation for why this change occurred, except for the fact that humans continued to push further and further into animal territory as their civilization expanded.

Humans had named the epidemic caused by these renegades the Severe Acute Respiratory Syndrome (SARS) epidemic of 2002. *The viral forefather of Q47cx, SARS, had realized that the best form of transmission from one human to the next is by respiratory spread. It could infect new hosts whenever they breathed or spoke or sang. Other viruses that had attempted to spread by other means, such as blood transfusion or exchange of bodily fluids, seemed not to fare as well. SARS understood that for maximum spread, the respiratory route was the only option. It knew that infection through casual contact was the only way to ensure that massive numbers of humans became sick. What it failed to realize is that—because respiratory spread usually occurs after symptoms are already present, or just shortly before symptoms appear—its enemy possessed a built-in advantage. Healthy humans had time to distance themselves from sick ones, thereby avoiding infection altogether. SARS had managed to cause serious illness, but through measures of isolation and social distancing, humans managed to defeat their viral enemy. Casualties and deaths were relatively small on a global scale.*

Comparing its job to that of human athletic teams it had long observed, SARS knew that scouting reports were invaluable. The human football quarterback Peyton Manning knew his opponents' defensive plays better than most of the defenders against whom he competed. So SARS decided that if its descendants were to have a truly devastating impact, it needed to generate better scouting reports and protect itself better.

Q47cx, plotting its revenge in 2019, had learned its lesson well from SARS. The new virus had changed its form to allow for easier transmission days before any symptoms occurred and, most cleverly, sometimes decided to produce no symptoms at all. Q47cx, like a covert operative behind enemy lines, knew that silence was of the essence. If humans were not even aware that they were infected and contagious, countless more individuals could be made ill. They would not even know who carried the virus and who did not. Scouting report: Remain quiet as long as possible. Spread but do not speak.

SARS had made its descendant aware of another mistake that led to its defeat. In order to bind to an enemy host cell and therefore infect it, a virus must first find a way to attach itself to the outside of the cell. Although SARS had found a way to do that, it was an unreliable method. Many times, the bond was not strong enough to hold on for long periods of time, and as a result, many host cells could not be destroyed. Q47cx learned how to hold on longer to the enemy by attaching itself tighter, so that it could infect cells at a much more efficient rate. Scouting report: Spend more time in the gym, strengthening the upper body. Make certain tackling is sure. Do not be so easily pushed away.

Q47cx was aware that it must become deadly while completely out of the sight of observing eyes. To perfect its craft, it must have a practice host that no one would notice. After making itself formidable in secret, it would then make the deadly jump to humanity. First it considered using dogs as its vector—its training ground—before realizing that the humans would immediately turn their attention to sick domestic animals. Veterinarians would quickly seize the opportunity to diagnose and treat the animals, as well as sequester them. Q47cx's fate would mirror that of SARS. It then considered livestock until it realized that any animal vector routinely exploited by humans for food would also be closely watched. Although some humans would become ill, the source of the food contamination would be quickly traced and the source efficiently shut down. Q47cx knew that to remain completely clandestine during its training phase, it had to go elsewhere. Somewhere dark, somewhere the humans were afraid to go.

Q47cx was sure that the reprehensible and repulsive nature of bats, in the eyes of the humans, made it the perfect training host. No one purposefully went near bats. If humans found one dead there would be no great motivation to find out why it died. Bats were usually swept up and discarded. Most of the humans were merely happy to have the carcass out of sight. In the bat, Q47cx could experiment with more lethal ways to kill. When the time came, it would make the jump to human hosts, and then it would be too late to neutralize the virus's finely-honed lethality.

Q47cx knew the challenges that lay ahead of it. The human immune system was formidable, and getting past human defenses was known to be a herculean task. Q74cx had learned the maneuvers by heart: Once a human host cell is infected with a virus, a protein called interferon sends out signals and instructions. The interferon signals other cells to release attack agents to destroy the virus and its deadly agenda. But Q47cx had figured out how to beat interferon. The answer to its threat was to produce decoys, so many, in fact, that they literally overwhelmed the system. To that end, Q47cx built structures into its gene complex that were three times the size of the flu virus genome. The additional structures in the genome were there to distract the *interferon, rendering its response less effective because it had too many tasks to perform. Scouting report: Overwhelm by sheer numbers.*

In the aftermath of its defeat, SARS had realized that it not only needed to win a physical war, but a psychological one as well. For this, it knew that it had to be patient. There was no rush. What, after all, was the difference between killing tens of thousands in 2008 as opposed to 2012 or 2017? The objective was maximum lethality, no matter how much time it took. Knowing that a well-coordinated world effort would seriously cripple its mission to spread throughout the entire populace, it waited. It waited for international travel to be second nature. More importantly, it waited for such political divisions and polarizations to take place that every item of news was hotly debated by at least half of the population. It waited until most people had a reflexive distrust of anything other than what the people in their political camp wrote or said.

Thus, Q47cx was able to spread virtually unchecked because each attempt to thwart its attack was met with resistance from other humans. It bred and spread as political arguments dragged on endlessly.

5

THE CANDY APPLE RED TOYOTA SUPRA SPRINTED AROUND THE corner and into the circular driveway of the reasonably well-appointed Tudor. The dynamic energy of the vehicle seemed to be an extension of its fiery driver. A very short natural hairstyle popped out of the driver's seat and yelled at the stately gentleman standing in awe on the front step.

"Hey Doc! Is M&M here?"

"Hi Lil Man," the professor replied. "She's around back."

The driver popped out and wagged a playfully chastising finger attached to a tiny, five-foot-two-inch young woman of 26, built like a gymnast.

M&M was the young driver's beloved former teacher, Mrs. McGuire. While Marnie had been finishing up her graduate course-work, she couldn't bear the thought of leaving the classroom and had continued to teach her beloved fourth grade as she wrote her doctoral dissertation. During that time, she finally changed her name to reflect her married status, at her husband's urging. But for a full year her students had trouble remembering she was Mrs. McGuire and not Miss Jackson. One day, a child made it easier on himself by calling her "Mrs. M," and all the other students followed suit. The perky little Supra driver, when she had been a fourth grader, shortened it to M&M.

And it just so happened that Mrs. McGuire adored M&Ms. Plain, no peanuts or almonds. No fancy ones. Just good ol' plain M&Ms. Sure enough, when Lil Man got out of her car, rattling in her pocket was her usual offering to Mrs. McGuire, picked up at a convenience store and duly decontaminated.

If M&M was a logical nickname, derived from Marnie's initials, the moniker "Lil Man" had arisen from a simple misunderstanding. One afternoon, after finishing at the lab, Professor McGuire had dropped by the grade school fifteen blocks away to see his wife. In the back of the room stood a diminutive student straightening chairs and desks. Upon entering the classroom, which always smelled of three-day-old oranges for some reason, Al met Marnie's warm gaze as she called out, "Hi! Meet one of my favorite students." An emergency siren began to blare as she continued, so that Al could only hear fragments of what she was saying. "This is Lil—Man—." Since the tiny student had a baseball cap pulled down over her long kinky locks, Al thought she was a boy. Under the impression that his wife was using a term of endearment, he responded, "Well, nice to meet you Little Man."

Marnie and Lillian roared with laughter as Al stood in shock.

"Wha—What did I say wrong?" he stammered.

"I said *Lillian Manning*," Marnie answered, with an exasperated eye roll.

Embarrassed, the professor blurted out, "I am sooo sorry!"

Lillian could not stop laughing, and the accidental nickname became an instant inside joke among the three of them.

More than a decade later, their Saturday afternoon ritual had become a favorite of the McGuires. Lillian couldn't wait to throw off her white coat and head home to tell M&M everything that had happened during the week. Yes, *home*. As a senior resident in the Department of Pediatrics at Pelican State Medical Center, Lillian led an extremely busy life, and her refuge, her home, was the guest wing of the McGuires' spacious Tudor. None of them had planned it that way.

As a final-year medical student, Lillian had decided to include Pelican State on the shortlist of teaching hospitals where she wanted to continue her medical training. She knew she would discover on Match Day whether one of the institutions on her list had selected her as one of its desired candidates. The nights leading up to Match Day were restless for Lillian. But when she finally opened her envelope at noon, she let out a small shriek of joy. Pelican State had included her on its shortlist, and Lillian would do her medical residency there.

When Lillian matched so close to home, the McGuires insisted that she live with them. Lillian objected at first but was soon persuaded by the fact that decent housing reasonably close to the hospital was terribly expensive. In addition, as a resident she would be returning home at extremely odd hours, so the safety of her neighborhood was crucial. She insisted on paying rent to the couple, and they consistently declined to accept it. Doing the math, Lillian concluded that her amenities and the relative security of the neighborhood would command at least twelve hundred a month. But she would accept a family discount. On the evening of every first day of the month, Lillian would write a check for nine hundred dollars and leave it on the kitchen table. On the morning of each second day of the month, Lillian would find an envelope with her name on it. Inside the envelope was her check, neatly cut into equal fourths, then reattached with a smiley-face sticker.

In virtually all ways M&M was a mother to her. Lillian had a complicated relationship with her own mother, who had been an exceptional dancer. Shortly after she had turned seventeen, Ellie Manning had become pregnant by a fellow student at her school, and her life was changed for good. She had been a fiercely talented dancer but, after giving birth to Lillian, never performed beyond community theater stages. Without the pregnancy, she could have gone on to great acclaim on the urban theater circuit. If Ellie had lived in a different age, however, she could have been a Broadway performer. At a lean five foot nine inches, with unworldly flexibility, Ellie would have made a wonderful

Rockette, or a solid member of just about any major dance company in New York. Her dancing prowess was widely known, but the deeply segregated South precluded any dreams of her performing on The Great White Way. That she had a daughter in tow made it difficult to find success even on the stages where she could legally perform. Instead she took entry-level clerical jobs as she and her husband, a much older leader of a jazz orchestra, struggled to make ends meet for their small family. Eventually her husband got tired of it all and picked up and left. But Ellie held tightly onto the dream that she would one day see her daughter fulfill her own frustrated ambitions.

That dream ended one Tuesday afternoon in a pediatrician's office. Ellie had taken Lillian for her eight-year check-up. Ellie had noticed that Lillian was already starting to have tiny breast buds and was puzzled. When the doctor finished the exam he said to his shy, polite patient, "You are going to be a little lady a little early." Then he turned to Ellie and explained, "It's not abnormal, but within the next year look for full development to occur. It's perfectly normal." Turning back to Lillian he said, "It just means according to this chart you will stop growing a little before most children."

"What does that mean?" Ellie asked, with her heart in her throat.

"It means she will be perfectly normal, with a height of about five feet two inches."

Lillian did not understand all of the words drifting between the two adults, but the look of disappointment that flashed across her mother's face was unmistakable. The image lodged itself permanently in her memory.

Before Ellie could catch herself, she blurted out "That short?"

"Well, Mrs. Manning, that's a normal height," the doctor replied.

But it was too late. Lillian already knew that she would never be what her mother really wanted.

Ellie felt dizzy, almost faint. Regardless of talent, who would hire a five-foot two-inch dancer for the big stages? Although she tried to reassure Lillian on the way home from the appointment that everything would be okay, the perceptive girl heard the hollow, brittle grief in her mother's voice. An innocence deep with in her died that day, and a dull sadness was born in its place. From then on, whenever Ellie lost her temper with her daughter, Lillian had the feeling that she was being blamed for something she had nothing to do with.

Years later, in a psychology class, memories of that eight-year check-up would visit Lillian like a ghost. "When a parent inadvertently reveals to a child that they can never be what the parent truly wants," the professor intoned, "something dies within the child. It isn't like when a parent wishes a child would dress better or perform better in school. Those are things a child can change. When the *unchangeable* is not good enough, a permanent mark is left deep in the soul of the child."

Beyond sadness, Lillian nursed a seething anger but—polite, obedient daughter and student that she was—never allowed it to emerge. Unaware that the anger smoldered beneath the surface, Lillian was forced to confront it on her second rotation in her internship year. It was an incident that earned her the first and only official reprimand of her otherwise stellar career. The rotation was outpatient pediatrics, in a clinic setting. As the junior resident, Lillian was required to begin the evaluation and then staff the patient with the senior resident, handing over the patient's care. She remembered the active little boy from his previous visits to the clinic with his grandmother, whose last nerve he was energetically working. Lillian gently asked him to sit down a few times, but he continued to bounce around the small examination room. Lillian, taking the history from his grandmother, largely ignored his romping. But it wasn't as easy for the grandmother. The dam finally burst when he pulled a heavy book from the shelf and dropped it loudly to the floor.

His grandmother exploded and said the vilest thing Lillian had ever heard a parent or grandparent say to a child. Grandma screeched, "Get over here and sit down you little bastard, nobody wanted you anyway."

Lillian's response was immediate and instinctive. Had she thought about it, she would have calmly made the elderly woman aware of her inappropriate language and advised her in proper child-rearing techniques. But she didn't. Instead, years of anger from never having been enough, through no fault of her own, were roiling within her like lava before a volcanic eruption. She exploded, "How dare you talk to him like that! Maybe if you had done your job you wouldn't be here with him now because his drug addict mother is too strung out to take care of her own child!" She instantly knew she had crossed the line. It was too late to take it back.

The senior resident, who had been observing near the door, stepped into the room and said, "Dr. Manning, may I see you for a minute outside?" The blistering reprimand came right there in the hallway. The senior resident finished examining the patient and dismissed Lillian for the afternoon.

The summons from the chairman of the department came the next morning. Lillian was asked to explain the incident. After hearing the story, Dr. Coachman looked over his glasses. He leaned back in his chair and asked, "What time are you scheduled for clinic today?"

"Nine o'clock," Lillian replied quietly.

"It's nine thirty. You're late. Go catch up. And remember, some truths must remain in the mind and not on the lips." He smiled at his intern and sent her to clinic.

———

In the fourth grade, when Lillian had met Mrs. McGuire, the weight of her sadness had transformed into something more buoyant and hopeful, but her anger still occasionally flared. Marnie had seen nothing but potential in the energetic little ten-year-old, always completing her work flawlessly before the rest of the class was halfway done with theirs. Mrs. McGuire even found herself bringing in extra work just to keep Lillian challenged. The precocious grade-schooler was already learning calculus and even developing a taste for physics and chemistry. Craftily, Mrs.

21

McGuire had learned to keep the challenging extra work away from the other children in the class. She was concerned that if Lillian's schoolmates knew that a fourth grader was delving into high school geometry, the potential for her to be bullied would rise exponentially.

The vigilant teacher had already seen glimpses of the way things could turn. Whenever Lillian had to make presentations in front of the class, she heard other students challenging her, "Why you talk white?" Although overhearing the question infuriated Marnie, she fully understood the origin and roots of it. She was well aware that, in a world where children are shown few academically successful role models that look like them, they come to see such success as beyond their reach. She knew that the broken English of her little ones' grandparents, as well as the careless English of their contemporaries, made the grammatically correct utterances of little black girls an oddity. Marnie deplored the fact that the only contact outside of school that most black kids had with correct grammar was with news reports and all-white television shows. The programs that did feature black casts mostly showed characters who only spoke dialect or slang.

Marnie would never forget the heated discussion that had taken place in the teacher's lounge one day when one of the guidance counselors made a comment about *The Cosby Show*. "He's a doctor and she is a lawyer," Carrie Sullivan said to one of her co-workers. "In what world are these children ever going to see that?"

The attack was swift and brutal but unsurprising to Marnie, given that Carrie had made it known on several occasions that she felt it was her mission to save poor little black children. Tired of the low expectations that some of the other teachers held for their students, Marnie decided to make an example of Carrie.

"Maybe ah be changin' mah lesson plans, Miss Sullivan," Marnie snarled in a made-up, deferential dialect. "Ah needs to make sho' ah be teachin' dem sumptin' dey can actually do. Ah shol is sorry dat ah dun gave dem de mind dat dey could evah be good as you is." The arctic chill in the room left everyone speechless.

Miss Sullivan, her complexion now matching the plum she was about to devour, turned and left the room.

As Marnie exited the room a few minutes later flushed with anger, she reflected on what had just happened. For the umpteenth time, she thought about how children, at their core, were affected by the expectations of the adults around them. Lower expectations always produced lower outcomes. Her mind wandered back to the contents of her graduate thesis, *The Overuse and Underuse of Stimulant Medication in Black Children, and Its Effects on Educational Success.* It was a topic that had intrigued Marnie from as far back as she could recall—how medications could be both overused and underused in the same population at the same time, depending on the expectations of the evaulating clinician.

Just as she had done with Miss Sullivan, Marnie had used her flair for the dramatic to begin her doctoral dissertation in a less formal style, to jar her readers into understanding that she was not discussing abstract ideas but human beings with beating hearts, aspirations, and ambitions. Marnie could see the opening pages of chapter 1 against the black backdrop of her closed eyelids.

Johnny is the child of a single mother who cleans hotel rooms for a living. His mother recognizes that he is incredibly smart. Every day she brings home the used newspapers from the rooms she has cleaned, and they read them together. Johnny is not only smart but well read and well versed. In the classroom, Johnny finishes his work in half the time required for the others and takes issue with statements the teacher makes that don't go along with what he read the night before. Since his teacher believes that it is not possible for a young black child to have this level of knowledge, he is seen as a troublemaker, and it is recommended that Johnny be medicated in order to control his "impulsivity." By contrast, his white counterpart brought up in the suburbs by two professional parents, who displays almost identical behavior, is praised for his abilities and given the label "gifted." Johnny is overtreated.

Marie is a quiet little girl who causes no trouble in class. One minute she sits quietly cutting out paper dolls; the next she hums a tune to herself and watches butterflies go by. Each time another child in the room moves or talks, she stops her work and peers over to see what they are doing. She eventually completes her assignments after being reminded to do them countless times. She is doing average work and making mostly Cs. Her teacher sees a little girl with a single mother who is passing in class, doing fine. What the teacher does not see is that despite her high distractibility, Marie can still make Cs. But what if she actually had the help she needed to stay on task? Marie has classic attention deficit disorder, but no one expects her to do better. Marie is undertreated.

Marnie's passionate thesis defense would go on be discussed by generations of students who followed her.

6

SINCE THE DISCOVERY OF Q47CX, THE VIRUS THAT HAD vaulted itself from bats to humans, Lillian had implemented meticulous precautionary measures for the McGuires' safety. Both Professor and Mrs. McGuire were awestruck by her nightly routine. No matter what time she arrived at home, Lillian would park the Supra and enter through a side door that led into an abandoned workroom with running water. In the workroom she had constructed a makeshift decontamination area. A shop light fluorescent fixture hung from the ceiling. Since the workroom had an industrial sink and a floor drain, Lillian had attached a hose to the industrial sink's faucet. There she ran a hose up the pegboard wall and fastened the hose to the wall with intermittently spaced zip ties. With a number of makeshift adapters she attached a showerhead to the end of the hose.

On entry to the chamber she would strip completely. There she would shower with relatively hot water and antibacterial soap. The moisturizing luxury soaps that kept her skin texture smooth were now risky indulgences. In their place, harsh antibacterial detergents left her skin with tiny cracks and fissure at the points of flexure. She combatted the dryness with various ointments, but the daily chemical bombardment still took its toll. Her once voluminous and bushy hair was now trimmed neatly to less than one-half inch in length. This allowed her to wash and scrub her scalp every night without fear of missing even one square millimeter. When she finished the shower, she would reach for a towel she had previously placed on the opposite wall the night before. She would place a clean towel there once she was decontaminated, never re-entering the small room until her subsequent return from the hospital. Also hanging on the "clean wall" were her "inside clothes." She would quickly re-dress in the hallway outside the small room. There was no fear of a privacy catastrophe, as Dr. McGuire never visited that side of the house. Only once she was decontaminated did Lillian feel comfortable interacting with her host family.

The surprise joyride for M&M had taken some planning. If Lillian drove to the house from the hospital, by definition she would expose Marnie to a contaminated car. She arranged for one of her older clerical confidants at the hospital—who worked only in the office and not on the patient wards—to deliver the car to a specific spot. Once Lillian was decontaminated, she would walk just a short distance down the road and retrieve it. Then she would drive back to the house and surprise M&M.

Full of devilish excitement, the athletic little whirlwind bounded up the front steps, right past the professor. Realizing her error, Lillian turned and quickly gave the older man a quick peck on the cheek before asking, "M&M here?"

Al merely rolled his eyes and nodded, knowing he would be a non-entity for the next hour or so.

"I got it, M&M! I got it!!" Lil screeched.

"You did *not* waste your money on that thing, did you?" the older woman scolded.

"It was a great deal! I worked emergency rooms three summers to get it! You have to go for a ride with me!"

Marnie was not accustomed to being dragged by the arm, but she allowed her beloved Lillian to do just that. Standing on her front step, Marnie gasped as she took her first look at the bright red Toyota Supra. "That's a race car!" Marnie exclaimed, feigning disdain. "What do you need with a race car?"

"It's not a race car, M&M. I bought it from the widow of a retired surgeon. He hardly ever drove it and kept it in the garage all year. When her husband passed away, she said she just didn't really want to see it anymore, so she practically gave it away! You have to go for a ride with me."

"Oh no!" Marnie protested. "You are not going to go zipping around with me in there."

Lillian laughed. "Come on, I want you to be my first passenger!"

The two women locked eyes for a moment.

What made Marigold Nelda Jackson such a fantastic educator was her ability to hear with her eyes. During her years of teaching she had heard the unspoken cries of abused children and acted on it. She had heard the unspoken requests for adequate food and had often fulfilled the need. She had heard the vicious jealousies of some of her coworkers when they spoke only with their crepe paper smiles. This time she heard the pleas of a young woman who just wanted to delight and thrill the mother figure in her life. "Ok Lil. Let's go," Marnie sighed.

Lillian's driving skills resembled those of a professional. Every available weekend she spent driving go-karts. Although it was a strange hobby for a pediatrics resident, go-karting relaxed her. Treating sick children often left Lillian drained and spent, but the speed and the wind of the go-karts allowed her to put her cares on hold just for a moment. Driving the most difficult courses, she would compare her times to the initialed but unnamed drivers atop the leader board. She consistently ranked in the top five and often saw her initials in the number one slot. It was as though she possessed otherworldly reflexes. When the go-kart tracks were closed, she would take her ancient Ford Probe—red of course—and drive around an abandoned parking lot in Metairie, just outside of New Orleans. Once a thriving retail center, the abandoned lot never reopened after Hurricane Katrina devastated the area. As there was rarely another car in sight, she would negotiate the dangerous poles and rocks, honing her civet-like reflexes.

Lillian adored autumn in Louisiana for its vibrant, multihued beauty, but she also knew that the price for all of that brilliance was capricious weather. M&M needed to be prepared for every meteorological eventuality on their ride. So Lillian gently guided Marnie back to the kitchen and commanded, "Put your *hair* on and let's go."

"Put your hair on" was not a slip of the tongue. Marnie was a twelve-year breast cancer survivor. The powerful chemotherapy had done its job, but the hair loss it caused remained permanent. There was thinning around the top and some growth in the back, but not to Marnie's liking. Marnie would never go out in public without one of her very well-crafted wigs. Only three people other than her clinicians had glimpsed her without a wig: her beautician, Al, and Lillian. Lillian was secretly proud of her admission to that elite club. Without saying it, Marnie had let her into a space few people would ever occupy. Lillian did not take her place of honor lightly.

Lillian remembered the first time she had seen Marnie after the initiation of the chemo, over twelve years previous. As a middle school student nearing high school admission, Lillian had been aware of cancer treatments but knew very little about them. She had begged her mother to go and see Mrs. McGuire, to take her a flower. M&M had been out sick for some weeks, and her favorite former student missed her terribly. Lillian's mother should have called first but didn't. Professor McGuire answered the door, momentarily confused to see a child holding an orchid, standing in front of a woman he'd never met. It slowly dawned on him that he was looking at Lil Man. He quietly explained that it really wasn't a good time.

Despite Al's efforts, Marnie was roused from a fitful sleep by her husband's voice. She weakly called out, "Who is it, honey?"

"Lil Man brought you a flower."

"Well, send her in!"

She struggled to hoist herself to a sitting position on the side of the bed and reached for a scarf to cover her head. At the same time, she tried to kick the small pail under the bed that was there to catch the results of the endless nausea caused by the drugs. As she heard the door open, the scarf slipped from her hand. There was no chance to retrieve it. Lillian stepped into the room, and her eyes were drawn to the balding head of her teacher, and the pale and gaunt face that stared back at her. But even at a young age, Lillian possessed a capacity for empathy well beyond her years. The eighth grader never commented. She simply ran to her former teacher and hugged her.

"We miss you Mrs. McGuire." Although she held it together well, Lillian's emotions were betrayed by the small tear that traced its way down her cheek.

She returned to her mother's car distressed. Lillian fought with the notion that she saw her teacher as more of a mom than her own mother. She loved her mother, but Ellie never smiled. She never laughed, except when men would visit. Lillian wondered as a young girl what she had done to bring on the sadness. Only later, as an adult, would she realize that the implosion of a dream causes two shockwaves. The first is a moving wall of grief that distorts the dreamer's spirit. The second is a swell of blame that crashes down upon the one held responsible for ending the dream. Until her last breath, Lillian would wonder if she was on the receiving end of that blame.

———

Marnie went to her dressing closet to retrieve her wig. Looking in her mirror, she fastidiously brushed every one of its curls as though she were attending a ball. Once she deemed herself ready for inspection, she walked to the front door, keen to feel fresh air on her face after so many weeks in lockdown.

After making her way down the front steps, Marnie walked around Lillian's new toy, inspecting every inch. "It *is* a race car, Lil," Marnie snorted, making the little sound with her lips as though she had just spit out a tiny fruit seed. Lillian opened the door to the passenger side and Marnie sat down. Looking particularly awkward, she complained, "I'm just about laying down in this thing!"

"Oh M&M, let me adjust the seat." Lillian raised the passenger seat three inches to the maximum height and asked, "Is that better?"

"Cabin doors locked and cleared for takeoff," Marnie chuckled.

Lillian turned the key and animated the powerful 3.0-liter, turbocharged, in-line, six-cylinder engine, waking up the 365 horses. So as not to make the professor or his wife nervous, she slowly pulled out of the driveway, gently creeping through the brick pillars that formed the entry way. When she had cleared the drive and was out of sight of the professor, she advised Marnie to "Hold on!"

The Supra, with its dual clutch transmission, was predatory in its assault of the road. As it sprang forward, Marnie gripped the seat and screamed "Lillian!!" in tones she often used with mischievous fourth graders. Lillian laughed and tossed her head back but refused to slow down. In Lil's mind, the kind, strait-laced former teacher just needed a little adventure every now and then. They headed for some back roads in farm country, to be free of the city traffic and annoying traffic signals. Lillian knew every back road from the hours of exploration she had logged, just curious to see where each pathway led. Some of the roads led to abandoned farms or other long deserted structures, while others led to nowhere. There were roads that featured long straightaways and others that boasted elaborate twists with hairpin turns. All were exhilarating. She checked her passenger but couldn't quite read M&M's expression. In fact, Marnie's face was stuck somewhere between "Bonding is wonderful" and "This child is going to kill us both!"

On one stretch of straightaway, a few patches of dense trees peeked out. Once the Supra reached an even cruising speed, Marnie managed to settle down a little. Then a small squirrel darted from one of the roadside bushes directly into Lillian's path. A nature lover, Marnie screamed, "Look out!!" Bracing herself for the sudden braking Lil was sure to do, Marnie tightened every muscle. What she felt was not braking, but exactly the opposite. Lillian coolly hit the gas. With a sudden acceleration and a slight snap to the oncoming lane, Lillian whizzed past. In the side rearview mirror Marnie saw the creature scamper away. "Lillian?" she asked with a perplexed gaze. "Why did you try and kill that little animal?"

Lillian smiled and said softly to her former teacher, "M&M, I wasn't trying to kill him. I was trying to save him. In the forest there are predators and prey, as you taught us in fourth grade. Squirrels are almost always prey, and hawks and bobcats feed on them frequently. Because evasion is their only chance to escape, they have to zigzag back and forth when they run away, in order to escape capture and death. The squirrel that ran out into the road just now was suddenly faced with a predator: us. So I knew his first move would be to run back to where he'd been safe only a few minutes before. Then his *next* move would be to run back, reversing his course. Evasion. But if I had slowed down, that reversal would have been deadly; he would have run right under my right front tire. My only chance to save him was speeding up. And by swerving, I moved out of the path where he would have been crushed by the tire. If I had hit the brakes, his timing would have been fatal. You know I would never allow that."

Then Lillian's tone became nostalgic. "Do you remember the mouse that got into our classroom?"

Marnie didn't answer but remembered the incident vividly.

"It took three days for Mr. Simmons to catch it. He was so proud to rid us of that creature. I still remember how the mouse trap snapped across the back of his neck. I cried for two days and insisted we take it outside and bury it."

Marnie would never forget the impromptu mouse funeral that had thrown her lesson plan into disarray that day. For weeks she thought Lil would never recover. She remembered thinking, "It's just a mouse for God's sake."

Lillian's soft voice brought her back to the present. "M&M, you know I can't kill things."

They breezed along quietly for a while, just enjoying the sights. Lillian and her surrogate mother. The mother who really didn't care how tall she was or whether she could dance. The mother that just loved her soul.

———

Q47cx continued to learn new ways of spreading. The fact that it was now able to spread from person to person without its hosts ever knowing they carried it was a tremendous advantage. Q47cx knew from its forefather SARS that when the humans wore masks, they mounted one of their most formidable defenses against viral infection. Although it had waited patiently until political divisions had reached a feverish peak, it could never have dreamed that these divisions would cause a huge swath of the human population to renounce wearing masks. Masks had become a political statement. Q47cx was ecstatic. The fewer masks the better. The non-mask wearing crowds declaring that no government would ever tell them what they could or could not do. Within each cough, sneeze or hearty laugh, when in range, the virus made its way to yet another host. Powerful political figures appeared without masks, inciting others to do the same. Q47cx's fear that its fate would mirror that of SARS ebbed as it watched huge crowds of humans screaming and protesting.

"Thank you, mankind," it thought.

7

UNLIKE MANY INDIVIDUALS AT THE TOP OF THEIR CHOSEN FIELD, Professor Alton McGuire had not feared retirement. On the contrary, he had been determined to avoid the fate of some of his most revered sports heroes who had stayed too long. Images of the great Willie Mays, arguably the greatest outfielder of all time, haunted Al. Watching number 24, "The Say Hey Kid" stumble through the outfield after a fly ball, or fail to get his bat around on a young kid's fastball, was painful. To then watch Muhammad Ali, who could no longer "float like a butterfly" or "sting like a bee," get pummeled by Larry Holmes, and later Trevor Berbick, was too excruciating. Al resolved to take an approach closer to the New England Patriots' Bill Belichick.

Because they had dominated the American Football Conference—if not the entire NFL—for more than a decade, the New England Patriots drew Al's unending ire. It was nothing personal, but they just won all the time. Even when they were losing, they would win. Skill was one thing, but skill *and* luck were just too much. The Patriots' secret lay in their coach Bill Belichick's ability to know just when to pull the plug on a player at the height of their powers.

How could someone know that the great year you just had was your last great year? Al wondered. The trajectory of a storied career is like a pendulum's, he thought to himself. It rises to the apex, then in just a split second, suddenly it is no longer rising but starting to fall. Most people wait until that downward slope is accelerating to decide to quit. But Belichick seemed to know exactly when a player's apex had passed and would promptly escort him to the door. Pure genius. Sure, as a Saints fan Al hated Belichick. But he recognized his genius.

There was a second reason Al had felt no fear toward the end of his academic career: retirement wasn't really retirement. The university allowed him to keep his lab—although he was moved to a non-academic research facility—and he continued to consult on various projects. He always said that continuing to work was good for him and helped him maintain the mental acuity he was known for. He interacted with a number of bright young scholars and was particularly impressed by the speed of new technology. Genome sequencing had been a laborious, painstaking process fifteen years before his retirement, but the current technology reduced it to an overnight triviality. Professor McGuire was known for making occasional references to "Scotty" and "warp drive" when referring to the speed of new technological advances. His references to the old television series Star Trek usually left the young geniuses around him with blank stares. To which Al would just mutter "Klingons!" and move on.

Friday afternoon was his favorite time. Unlike the days when he was publishing prolifically and rushing to meet end-of-week deadlines, retirement Fridays were relaxed. Al could leave the lab a little early and head to the grocery store. He did all of the grocery shopping. As soon as the virus hit, he absolutely forbade Marnie from venturing into supermarket aisles. On this particular Friday, Al left his lab, bitterly noticing that despite his early departure, he was still the last one there on a Friday. "Youngsters," he sighed to himself. He drove the five-mile trip to the largest of three supermarkets in the area. Although the prices were similar at all three, Al was a creature of habit and knew where everything was at the biggest store, which cut at least forty-five minutes off of his shopping time. He did not enjoy wandering through aisle after aisle looking for the ridiculous place the grocer had placed the applesauce. That was decidedly not his cup of tea.

He pulled his well-used Ford Explorer into the parking lot and noted there were quite a few more cars than usual. There had been a run on all types of groceries since the pandemic had been announced, and Al was seeing it before his eyes. Even though he suspected the shelves would be empty, he tried the toilet tissue and disinfectant aisles first. His predictions were well-founded. Nothing this week. But he wasn't worried because he had an adequate supply. Al had predicted how his fellow man would behave during this unprecedented health crisis. He knew that the great communal cordiality would wither like the leaves in the fall, as the doctrine "every man for himself" ushered in survivalist hoarding. Before firm limits were placed on the purchase quantity, hoarders would literally buy eighty or a hundred rolls of toilet tissue. Amused, Al would reason, "Well if it gets that bad there will be no food. And if you can't eat you won't shit!" He kept his thoughts to himself, knowing that Marnie would scold him for his crass language.

Professor McGuire adjusted his N95 mask and went about his way. The N95 was a leftover from his laboratory days. At one time, he had had cases of them just stuffed in the closet. Through the years he had used most of them but still had a few remaining. Masks had become a hotbed issue. Although not everyone had a high-quality mask like the N95, a simple cloth face covering was adequate to decrease the spread of viral particles wafting through the air in tiny droplets of vapor by 75 percent. What was the big issue? A full-blown pandemic was sweeping the planet; people were dying, and its citizens had been asked to put on a mask in public places. The outcry was mind-boggling. People shouting about their freedoms being taken away and incessant contentious arguments about medical exemptions. For years, Al mused, there had been signs on every restaurant door, bakery, or grocery store: "No Shoes, No Shirt, No Service." But Al could never remember scores of angry barefoot, shirtless protestors screaming to be let in.

At first Al thought the resistance to mask wearing was just because people did not understand the scientific reasoning. But once public announcement after public announcement had clearly stated in simple language that wearing a mask protected the next person, the mask wearer's neighbor, Al realized the issue was deeper than that. He was frightened because the discovery that carriers could be asymptomatic had changed the narrative. If the virus could be spread even if you were well, then it was not enough to stay inside if you were sick. Everyone needed to wear masks. Al racked his brain to try to understand some people's refusal. The protection of everyone, especially high-risk individuals, was obviously the humane thing to do. Some of the vile rhetoric was repulsive.

"If old people can't take care of themselves, they should stay home."

"If they catch the virus and don't recover, that's survival of the fittest."

"If we all get it, our herd immunity will be better."

As the discourse grew louder on the national stage, Al's anger grew exponentially. While he hurriedly shopped, he noticed young men and women, one after another, with no masks. Occasionally he also saw an older person who was maskless. The vast majority of people without masks, however, were young, healthy-looking men. He thought angrily to himself, How many people did you infect today? You young and entitled fools, thinking the world belongs to you and you are free to do with it as you wish. He watched as a young, maskless man carefully placed a soda can in the recycling bin. How ironic, Al thought. This youngster would go through such pains to save the planet for future generations but did not see the value in putting a mask on to save the inhabitants of the earth now. He tried to calm himself each time he went grocery shopping, but the rank selfishness of the maskless crowds made his blood boil. The smug looks on their faces, and the disdaining glances they gave to him and his N95 did not help. "What a society," Al snorted.

Halfway down an aisle, he hung back for a few minutes to check his brands. Checking brands was very important because Marnie was completely hooked on particular brands. Whenever he would make an error and bring home the wrong brand of an item, she had her own unique way of addressing it. "Oh! They were all out of Delmonte green beans," she would smile and say. Or, "They just can't seem to keep those Green Giant peas in stock," as she looked at the generic brand he had purchased. It was futile to protest. He would say, "You didn't tell me to get that brand," and she would pleasantly respond, "It's ok, maybe I forgot."

"But you really didn't say a brand. You just said green beans, and these were a lot cheaper."

"I said I must have forgotten."

They would go back and forth for a few minutes until Marnie turned, smiled and said, "Decaf." And that was that. Throwing up his hands, Al would feign exasperation and walk away.

Al was pleased to see it looked like all of his brands were in order. With his mask secured, he approached the checkout register. He probably had few enough items to go through the self-service register, but each time he tried, the electronic voice would advise him to scan something he had already scanned, or place the item back in the cart, or some other generally annoying directive. He waited his characteristic eight feet from the customer in front of him. Public health guidelines demanded six feet, but Al liked to add a buffer. As he approached the cashier, he noticed that the young kid who looked like he was still in high school did not have his mask in place. Instead it hung at least an inch below his nose. Store policy required all employees to wear a mask, but he had devised his own creative way to rebel. As Al moved toward the register, he noticed the young man smirking.

"Oooh N95," he chuckled.

Al nodded slightly, ignoring the implied derision.

"You know this is all a hoax, right?"

With a puzzled look Al answered, "A hoax?"

"Sure! There is really no viral pandemic. This is just a political game."

My God, not another one, Al thought.

ERIC A. YANCY, MD

For some reason, Al believed the encounter could be a teaching moment for this kid. Al knew he was thinking, "Surely this old black man could use my much more informed perspective." The two looked at each other for a minute and the professor indulged his desire to educate.

"What about all the deaths that have occurred so far?"

Unbothered, the young man replied, "Have you seen 'em?"

This rejoinder functionally ended the conversation. The professor recalled the words of Mark Twain: "Never argue with a fool. Onlookers may not be able to tell the difference." This child, whose last science class was likely leaf collecting, thought he was going to bestow much needed wisdom on a poor old black guy burdened with his useless mask. Without another word, Al collected his groceries and headed toward his Explorer.

As he slowly walked through the parking lot, momentarily forgetting where he parked, he reminded himself of his surefire system. Yes, he was twenty degrees northwest of the "o" in the word "store" on the marquee. He moved one aisle over and went straight to the vehicle.

Historic sayings were always popping into Al's head at times like this. *He who knows not and knows not that he knows not is a fool; shun him.* If it were not against the law, Al might handcuff the lad with a few of his friends and make him sit for a day or so in the hospital's intensive care unit. There he would witness the "hoax" firsthand. Though Al had only seen glimpses of it on the evening news, Lil Man had told him in great detail of the suffering she observed on a daily basis.

Because all of the viral units were closed, there were no visitors at all. Clad in full personal protective equipment, the staff resembled aliens in a science fiction movie. Sealed "death gurneys," rarely seen in regular times, seemed to be everywhere. The saddest part was the loneliness. Lil had explained the hospital's protocols to him. If an infected person became sick enough at home, they would be brought to the emergency department. Once screened for their severity of illness, they would be admitted to the inpatient ward. In many cases this was the last physical contact they would ever have with a loved one. Married couples of thirty and forty years were forced to say goodbye for the very last time in the hallway of a hospital. In some cases, mechanical ventilation was the only way to try and salvage the precious remnants of their unfinished lives. Often, the last face they were to see in this lifetime was the face of the intensivist injecting the deep sedative and paralytic agent that facilitated their intubation.

The "hoax" alluded to by this naïve young conspiracy theorist was in fact the total destruction of families, the loss of marriages, and the inability to ever say goodbye to grandma or grandpa. iPads were provided in many units as the only way family members could communicate with their sick loved one. But, as each beleaguered, overworked medical worker knew, there is no way to wipe away a tear on the screen of an iPad. Come with me, young man, Al wanted to implore, as I show you the realities of life and death. There is no reset button. There is no credit card on file for you to purchase a few new lives. There is only the sadness of the infirm, mingled with the blood, sweat, and adrenaline of the caretakers, as despair sits perched in every room like an airborne carnivore waiting out the fatigue of its prey.

Sometimes Lil Man would come to the house and just cry. Marnie would be so broken up because there was no way for her to help. She would quietly let Lil sit there and cry. That's why Lillian had bought the red Supra. She could fly through country roads allowing the grief, anxiety, guilt, and pain blow off her like the leaves huddled on the windshield on a lovely fall day. Pediatrics was all Dr. Lillian Manning had ever wanted to do. But now she was called to duty in overcrowded units who just needed a body. Turning the Explorer ignition key, Al wondered how many others were just like that kid, unwilling to sacrifice just a little, on the outside chance that someone else would avoid death. From where on earth did these people and their egocentric opinions originate? If that kid heralded the compassion of tomorrow, God help us all.

8

SPORTSMAN'S PARADISE WERE THE WORDS EMBOSSED ON
nearly every Louisiana license plate back in the fifties. They had certainly
been there on the very first car the professor remembered, a green and
white 1955 Chevrolet Bel Air. It was the family car and reasonably well-
equipped for that time. There was no air conditioner, but the windows
rolled down and allowed a cool breeze on those hot Louisiana days. A sun
visor—an added extravagance back then—sat above the windshield. The
visor resembled the bill of a baseball cap, jutting out from the top of the
forward glass. In a moment of nostalgia, Al remembered his older sister
asking their father, "Daddy, why does the car have bangs?" There was a
roar of laughter, but it was years before Al figured out why it was so funny.

Al was always reminded of the slogan on the Bel Air license plate
whenever he went to Carson's Bayou, an idyllic body of water that was,
in fact, a sportsman's paradise. Though not very large, Carson's Bayou
had become a favorite spot for Al and his regular fishing buddy Charles
Carter. Every Saturday morning like clockwork, Al and CC—as he
was called by everyone close to him—would spend hours in paradise.
Dr. Carter was a brilliant biochemist. Having practiced medicine for a
number of years, he decided to return to school at the age of thirty-six

to pursue a PhD. As an endocrinologist, CC had been drawn to bio-chemistry, and he developed an extraordinary proficiency in the subject. His clinical skills gave his students insight into how the bonds and molecules they were studying would later be useful in the lives of ordinary people. The two men had met at a regional conference and became fast friends. Living in different cities, the two began meeting once a month for a fishing excursion. For all of its ceremony, the trip often yielded no fish. Still, the two men enjoyed each other's company and came to depend not only on the monthly ritual but also on the friendship whose bonds strengthened each month, forged through common struggles as scientists and husbands.

The beauty of Carson's Bayou was astounding. If a fisherman got there early enough, he could see the sun rising and reflecting off the bayou just like a picture postcard. The sounds of the bayou rivaled its images. Discordant tones of the multispecies orchestra were strangely hypnotic in the early morning hours. Al suddenly felt his face flush as memories from another time floated into his consciousness. He had not always been so enamored with the outdoors.

Twenty years previous, Al had been working sixteen hours a day, teaching a full course load and heavily involved in a demanding research agenda. The pressure to publish had taken its toll, and he was teetering on the edge of a mental collapse. He became angry at the slightest provocation and met Marnie with frosty silence whenever he returned home, usually after midnight.

One night after Al had worked forty hours straight, CC decided to drop by his old friend's lab. He had gleaned from their fishing trips that Al was distracted and feeling distant from Marnie, and he felt compelled to intervene before it was too late. CC handed Al a box of pralines.

Al looked at him quizzically.

"This is for Marigold."

Out of nowhere, Al exploded, enveloping the room like an enormous blue flame on a propane stove, lit by a spark after too much gas has escaped the canister. He screamed, "What are you trying to do Charles? Make me look bad in front of *my wife?* Who the hell do you think you are?"

CC was stunned. He had never seen his friend like this. Who was this maniacal lunatic? With a jolt, CC realized Al was suffering from extreme burnout; he had witnessed it enough times during his years as an endocrinologist. He knew what needed to be done. Slowly, he walked over to Al and closed his notebook.

Al jumped up and shouted in CC's face, "Are you crazy!? I'm working here!"

CC felt the thump of his heartbeat as he sensed the rage in Al's balled up fists and clenched jaw. Realizing they were about to come to blows, CC took a deep breath and quietly responded, "Not anymore. You are done for the night."

CC drove his car right behind Al's, all the way back to the Tudor. When they arrived, CC placed the box of pralines on the table, as Marnie had already gone to bed. "We will talk tomorrow," CC said. "I will be here in the morning at five thirty. Yes that's a.m. Wear jeans and a long-sleeved shirt. We're going fishing."

Al protested vociferously, in a stage whisper. "Are you crazy? How can I go fishing with eight weeks of work to do and only three weeks to do it?"

CC stood firm. "You can't afford *not* to go," he spat. "Look at you! You're a mess! Yelling at everyone. You don't even talk to Marnie anymore."

"Stay out of my home life!"

"I won't stay out of it as long as you're like this. You and Marnie deserve better."

"Oh, so it's about *Marnie* now?" Al snarled. The mammoth blue flame reappeared in an instant, larger and more menacing this time, incited by the propane of Al's suspicion that CC wanted Marnie for himself. How in the hell did he remember that pecan pralines were her favorite? The thought of Marnie with CC set off an inferno inside Al, and he picked up a glass from the table and fired it into the dormant fireplace.

The two men stared at each other, faces burning.

Wrapped tightly in a housecoat, Marnie raced into the room in a full panic and screamed, "What is going on in here?"

Realizing they had woken her from a deep sleep, Al and CC were shaken out of their outrage. Al squeezed his eyes tightly. What had he allowed himself to do, to become? CC was the best friend he'd ever had, and likely would ever have. He shook his head and sat down.

CC quickly righted the ship. "Hey Marigoooold." CC always teased her, dragging out the final syllable of her name. "We were just talking about fishing and I accidentally tossed this glass trying to show Al a new casting maneuver. I tried to catch it but missed. I am so sorry."

Marnie looked at the two men. She shook her head, turned around, and went back to bed.

Al looked at CC with remorse, silently waving the white flag. "Four hours, man. That's all I got."

"Four hours is all you need," CC said. He walked over and put his hand on his friend's shoulder. "I'll be here at 5:15."

9

AL WALKED DOWN THE LEVEE TO THE WATER'S EDGE carrying his bamboo fishing pole. CC, the experienced fisherman, carried two rods, various items in a fully stocked tackle box, and of course his characteristic fishing vest worn by sports magazine models. He laughed at Al for his minimal gear, but Al didn't mind. The last thing he needed to do was fuss over fishing gear. Seeking a respite from CC's teasing, Al's mind drifted back to another bayou fishing trip decades earlier.

When Al was ten years old, he had gone fishing for the first time with his grandfather. Both his grandfather and his grandmother were avid fishers, and as soon as Al was old enough to go, they took him along with them. They always left extremely early with brown bag lunches, and that particular day Al was beaming with pride that he had packed his own lunch. Al rode with his brother in the back of their grandparents' old pickup truck, seated on a little bench. No modern seatbelt or restraints of any kind. Only open-air fun. The very first time he had ridden with his Grandma and Grandpa, he must have been five or six, but he didn't fish, so it didn't count. The day he packed his own lunch and cast his reel for the very first time? That day counted. Grandpa always carried a four-foot piece of rod he called his snake rod. Later Al

44

came to learn the technical name was *rebar*, but snake rod remained his preferred name for the pole.

On Al's eleventh birthday, his grandfather, much to the indignation of his mother and father, gave him a shotgun. His grandfather argued that one day he would take his grandson hunting, so Al needed to be ready, didn't he? The firearm was a Winchester 410-gauge, single shot shotgun. Al thought it was the most beautiful thing he had ever seen. His grandfather would take him to distant fields and deserted country roads and let him shoot it. The first time he pulled the trigger the recoil nearly knocked him down, but he enjoyed it. He begged his grandfather to take him shooting whenever he could. With a few months' training, Al became pretty proficient hitting cans and other small targets. He would look down the beaded sight and pull the trigger. Once Al learned how to squeeze the trigger, stabilizing his aim, he could send the Coke cans flying at forty, then fifty, then seventy-five yards.

Al's grandfather always let him take his shotgun fishing just in case they came across any snakes. Al carried three shells with him all the time. He never thought he would actually get to use them, but he was determined to be ready. Only once did he and his grandfather encounter a snake who posed any kind of threat, but the memory had etched itself permanently in Al's mind.

As soon as the young fisherman became a little more proficient at baiting his own hook and no longer got the Eagle Claw hook stuck in his hand, Grandpa would let him wander down the banks of the bayou maybe forty or fifty yards away to fish on his own. No worries at all, not like modern grandparents, the professor chuckled to himself. About mid-morning, eleven-year-old Al, settling in to watch the cork bobber float lazily on the water, heard his grandfather shout, "Al! come here and bring your gun." Al immediately got up and ran with his unloaded shotgun toward his grandfather. When he was a short distance away his grandfather called out, "Stop!"

Al stared at his grandfather with his eyebrows raised.

"Snake. Big one."

Al's glance followed the path of Grandpa's gaze.

"Cottonmouth," Grandpa said. "I thought I could get him with my rod. I missed him earlier."

Apparently, Grandpa had taken at least one swipe at the snake with his snake rod, but the cottonmouth had evaded the blow. It looked like a standoff.

"Can you get him?" Grandpa asked.

Al didn't answer but reached in his button-up shirt pocket and took out a shell. He hurriedly breeched the shotgun and put the shell into the small chamber. Locking it back up he took aim, the gun unsteady in his trembling hands, and fired. The snake snapped his head around. Definitely not hit, Al thought bitterly. He listened intently for the rustling in the leaves but could not place it. Al's frustration mounted as the cottonmouth continued inching toward his grandfather.

He hurriedly reloaded the smoking shotgun, and the spent shell popped out as he broke it down. He placed the second shell in, caught a flash of snakeskin several yards from his feet, and fired. The bullet missed the snake again, but by a far smaller margin. The large reptile, now sensing danger, moved even closer to Al's grandfather, who backed up until he was up against a large tree. By now Al had ejected the second shell and had chambered the third and final shell. The cottonmouth crawled over a rotting log no more than four feet from his grandfather and coiled. A strange calm gripped Al as he watched the snake come menacingly close to his grandfather, this time in a tight corkscrew. His grandfather was still. Al stared straight ahead at the snake. The world slowed down. Nothing existed except his .410 shotgun and the potential assassin of his beloved grandfather. With icy proficiency, Al raised the shotgun with strangely steady hands, placed the head of the snake on the bead of the shotgun sight, and pulled the trigger. The coiled snake remained, his head surgically removed as though on a dissecting table in a herpetology lab. Al stood frozen for a second, still holding the shotgun in the firing position.

Al was surprised by what he felt afterwards. He had expected to feel bad. When his parakeet died, he had cried for hours. In fact, he bawled whenever a kitten, puppy, or hamster he knew of met an untimely death. His brother and sister teased him without end because he agonized for days after hearing fairy tales in which fictional creatures suffered or died. Yet he was completely at peace, having killed the menace to the one he loved. There was satisfaction, and no remorse. He walked over to inspect the remains of the snake.

"Good shot," his grandfather said. "Good shot, Al!"

His feelings churned inside him. It had indeed been a good shot, but he had taken it with emotional coldness. A vacuum in his soul had been replaced with the overwhelming desire to protect and to kill if necessary. There was no anger toward the snake. He had simply been determined to destroy it because it had threatened his grandfather. The feeling made him uneasy. It was a feeling his eleven-year-old mind could not process, complete satisfaction with eliminating a threat. He put it away in a private drawer in his consciousness, not anxious to bring it out again.

Professor McGuire stared out at the bayou. He intently watched his cork bobber. It suddenly disappeared below the surface of the water. It did not skim, or dance, or go back and forth. The bobber just disappeared. From all the hours on the water with his grandfather, Al knew what was on his hook.

"Catfish!"

10

"FISHING SATURDAYS" WEREN'T JUST FOR THE GUYS. M&M and Lil loved them too. Shortly after Lillian moved in, she and Marnie had settled into a fun Saturday ritual. Lillian would get up quite early for her big workout. Usually the men had only been gone an hour or so. She would sneak into the spacious family room, turn on the big screen television, and tee up one of her workout videos saved in the DVR. Then she would mute the sound and exercise in bare feet, so as not to awaken Marnie. After an hour of high intensity workout of stretches, dance moves, and calorie-burning aerobics, Lillian would be sweaty but happy. She prided herself on staying in perfect physical condition, but of course she had no time for a gym. So she worked out virtually during the week whenever she could, saving her big workout for Saturday mornings. Afterward she would go back to her room, shower down the hall, and dress in her comfortable Saturday clothes. Another hour would pass, and she would slowly turn up the volume on the television, causing Marnie to stir.

A bleary-eyed Marnie would walk into the room and scold, "You up already? You need more sleep than that." Feigning a yawn, Lil would say, "Oh I just got up a minute ago." Marnie recognized but never acknowledged the white lie, and both women would suppress a giggle at their silliness. Marnie would then return to her bathroom, wash her face, and head to the kitchen. That's when the real talking would begin.

The two women would trade off making various parts of the breakfast, an elaborate choreography that kept them in close contact. They each finished their contributions to the meal at about the same time so they could enjoy breakfast together. Marnie would say the grace prayer over the breakfast, and immediately follow with her ritualistic admonition, "And don't eat so fast this time."

It was good advice, and Lillian would try to make herself slow down. But M&M just did not understand the rigors of a residency program. Lil had learned in her first year: Either you eat fast or you don't eat. On one of her first call days she was too busy to eat a decent breakfast, so she scarfed down some juice and a bagel. At lunchtime she had two conferences and a ton of lab work, so she skipped lunch altogether. Almost weak with hunger by six o'clock in the evening, she dragged herself to dinner in the hospital cafeteria. The line wasn't long, so she took her time selecting every dish she wanted. As she sat down, she realized she'd forgotten extra napkins. Returning with the serviettes, she remembered she needed a bottle of water. After two false starts, she was relieved to sit down in front of a tray full of food. She happily diced the grilled chicken and sprinkled it over the fresh green salad. She closed her eyes and took a bite. Absolutely delicious.

"CODE BLUE, WARD B, PEDIATRIC SERVICE," the intercom blared. It was Lil's team. She was up. Dinner was over after only one bite. She learned her lesson that day. Now Lillian could get a full meal down in five minutes flat, despite Marnie's admonition ringing in her ears.

In addition to what Lillian called "turbo-meals," there was also "turbo-sleep." Because of her unrelenting resident's schedule, Lillian had learned to get to sleep very quickly. "No deep thinking once your head hits the pillow," she would remind herself. "And be ready to hit the ground running when your eyes open." She'd quickly realized the importance of waking up fully alert. If a call about a serious problem came at 3:20 a.m., she had to be fully alert to answer the question and then be able to go right back to sleep, or else the night's rest would be lost with no way to make it up. It had taken Lil a couple of months to master "turbo-sleep," but—like everything else she set her mind to—she had gotten the hang of it.

That first unpredictable year had been full of lessons. On Lillian's first trauma rotation as a relatively new intern, a call had come in during the late afternoon on a Saturday. Severe trauma to a fifteen-year-old who had been attacked by a Louisiana black bear. When the rescue squad arrived, life support measures were already in progress. The young man was taken to a trauma room and uncovered as his doctors needed to have access to all areas of his body. The sight was ghastly. Lillian stifled an urge to cry out. The shocking condition of the teenager was difficult to take even for physicians much more experienced than a first-year resident.

In severe shock, the patient was an ashen color. A large clear tube was taped in place, providing ventilator support for his respiratory effort. He was barely recognizable because his features were distorted by blood and torn flesh. Heavily sedated, the young man was perfectly still. Lillian's trance was cut short by the barking of the senior resident. The seasoned trauma surgery resident took complete charge. With his straggly blond hair haphazardly tucked under a surgical cap, he sounded like a quarter-back barking audibles.

"Call the blood bank and get me six units each of fresh frozen plasma and packed cells. Get the dopamine running and I need those lines wide open. You," he said pointing at Lillian, "get me an intraosseous line in place *now*."

Interns did not have names. To a senior trauma resident, an intern was just "you." The intraosseous line was the first Lillian had ever placed. She knew that the young man's veins were collapsed and that the only way to get effective fluids inside his body was to literally puncture the bone and place the fluids directly into the bone marrow space. Space within bone does not collapse and would be able to accommodate the fluids. She hesitated for a second and earned the full wrath of the surgeon. "You! Either get that line in or get the hell outta here!"

Lillian looked around frantically just as she felt a firm hand on her arm. The expert trauma nurse handed her the intraosseous set with the long, sharp needle needed to pierce the bone. She had observed the procedure but had never done one. The constant residential cry of "See one, do one, teach one" echoed in her head. With a shaky hand she plunged the needle into the bone of the lower leg.

"You got this," the trauma nurse said to her.

With the needle inserted, fluids poured into the bone marrow space. The young man did not improve.

The entire scene was unfolding rapidly as the teen fought for his life. The extremely elevated heart rate on the monitor showed that his heart was failing. It was trying hard to pump enough blood but losing ground.

The shrill voice of the second year resident shouted "V-fib!"

The young man's heart was not keeping up and had gone into an erratic rhythm with no chance of pumping blood effectively.

"Compressions!"

The next resident assumed a position over the bed and began cardiac compressions. The trauma from the attack was severe, and apparently there was blood accumulation in the chest cavity that prohibited effective compressions. The young man's heart rhythm did not change.

"Going open," the trauma surgeon shouted.

The nurse provided him with a new tray of instruments including huge scissors and clamps. With the intraosseous line now in place, Lillian had a chance to watch as the trauma surgeon made large cuts on either side of the patient's chest and opened his chest cavity. Then he began the internal cardiac massage. Placing both hands inside the chest cavity, the surgeon directly massaged the heart. Such a maneuver was generally a heroic effort, a last-ditch attempt to save a patient's life. Lillian could see that the mutilated young man was slipping away. One hour later, despite the best efforts of the trauma team, the young man died from his injuries.

Lillian had dealt with death during medical school but never in such a heartbreaking way. Although she had understood she would have to learn to deal with tragedy on many levels, the senseless death of someone so young hit her particularly hard. She walked out of the trauma room and took a seat in a quiet area down the hall. The senior resident took up the responsibility of handling the notifications, and even all the way down the hall, Lillian heard the excruciating cries of the young man's family and friends.

As she sat contemplating the horror of the whole situation, once again she felt a firm hand on her shoulder. It was the same nurse who had helped her through the intraosseous line placement. She moved around and sat in front of Lillian.

"First time?" she asked.

"Yes," Lillian replied.

"It will get better."

Lillian searched her kind face, incredulous but grateful for the comfort.

"I'm Stacey," the slightly older woman said. "I've been here for five years and it doesn't get any easier. You just get more used to it."

In the months that followed, and over the subsequent years, Lillian and Stacey became quite close. They discovered that they shared a common interest in old movies, so they tried to get together for old movie marathons once a month, alternating at each other's places. Lillian was thankful for the companionship. Although her mother's disappointment had left a dull ache in her heart, Lillian knew that she was lucky to have not one but two older women in her life who cared for her in ways she treasured. Stacey's trusted friendship at the hospital and Marnie's strong maternal presence at home made all the difference to Lillian's happiness.

Lil and M&M cherished their Saturday morning routine together, but the virus had changed all of that. With longer call schedules and shorter breaks, Lillian and all of the other residents were exhausted. Her Saturday morning ritual with M&M was forced to take a temporary back seat. Such was the case this Saturday morning. Post call, Lillian was in a death-like sleep, completely oblivious to the sounds of Dr. McGuire and CC leaving for a day on the bayou. Marnie had gotten up on her own and realized Lillian's usual television alarm had not woken her. Later she would learn that Lillian had gotten in at 4:15 a.m. and crashed immediately after decontaminating herself. There would be no breakfast chat this morning. Lil would likely be asleep until at least noon.

Marnie stealthily moved through the kitchen to prepare her own breakfast. Nothing elaborate today. Just a scrambled egg, two pieces of Hormel center cut bacon—Al had finally gotten the right brand from the store—and a slice of whole wheat toast. A small glass of grapefruit juice finished the meal. Marnie had craved grapefruit juice during months of her chemotherapy because the doctors had deprived her of it, saying that grapefruit juice interfered with one of the chemotherapeutic agents. Once off of that agent, she had made up for lost time. Al playfully called it yuck juice but was always careful to get the right brand.

After breakfast, Marnie figured she would get a head start on Sunday dinner. She checked the refrigerator for the honey crusted turkey slices. A full turkey had been too large for them for quite some time and was a waste of money. A local store provided already sliced, honey crusted turkey and Al was fine with that. She went to the cabinet to take out a can of corn for a corn casserole but suddenly recalled that Al had specifically requested a sweet potato casserole. No problem. She placed the corn back on the shelf and reached behind it for a can of candied yams. Pulling out the yams, she instinctively looked at the stenciled portion on the bottom of the can. *Best if used by* ... Oh dear, she thought. The yams had expired three months ago. Even though they were probably still good, she would not risk it. She opened the can, dumped the yams down the garbage disposal, and then rinsed the empty can, placing it quietly in the recycling bin.

Marnie now faced a dilemma. She wouldn't dare wake Lil for something silly like going to the store, and Al would likely not be home until after six o'clock. Al was strongly opposed to her going out, but she had no choice. After all, he had left her the N95 masks and she knew every precaution by heart. Don't stand too close to people. Don't have extended conversations, and don't touch your face. In addition, when the idiots with no masks come down an aisle, go the other way if you can. The mask is not for you; it's for them. But always keep yours on anyway. At least there will be one barrier between you and them.

Marnie lifted the keys to her 2015 Volvo S60 off the hook and dropped them in her purse. She ran to the closet in the bedroom and removed the N95 mask hanging on a now retired skirt hanger, putting it carefully in her purse. Then she placed her wig on her head and deftly straightened it. After a quick, exacting inspection of herself in the mirror, she headed for the door.

11

THE BIG BEAR GROCERY PARKING LOT RESEMBLED THE LOT of a sports arena. On a Saturday morning there were cars everywhere. Marnie had not remembered it ever being this busy. Each new report of the virus' lethality brought waves of panicked individuals to the stores to buy whatever was left on the shelves. She wondered whether her trip would end in futility. Marnie carefully placed the mask over her mouth and nose, careful to keep the elastic straps on her neck and not on the lower part of her wig. She wanted a good snug fit, as the masses were out in full force. The trip shouldn't take long, she reasoned, because she knew exactly where to find the yams. Making her way across the parking lot, she saw dozens of young people, and a few older ones, maskless. Inwardly she felt a surge of disapproval and the impulse to voice an objection, but she kept quiet, not wanting to provoke any retaliation.

The whole mask uproar seemed strange to Marnie. As a grade-school teacher, she had been teaching children for years to sneeze into their elbows. Curious about why the recommendation had changed from "cover your mouth," she'd investigated and found that any way you sliced it, the human hand could not adequately restrict the transmission of germs.

Fascinated, she had read that some scientists estimate the average velocity of a sneeze to be about six meters per second. Most people, and certainly grade school children, leave their noses uncovered when they cover their mouths, so a significant amount of spray would still exit the nose. Even if the public could somehow be trained to place a hand vertically in front of the face, a dubious proposition, significant amounts of spatter would still seep out at the corners of the mouth. But the elbow easily covers the mouth and nose and, because the head moves downward into the elbow, whatever the elbow doesn't catch is directed to the floor, away from other faces. Plus an elbow works even when the cougher or sneezer has their hands full with Play Doh or building blocks. Or cans of baked beans.

Marnie's attention snapped back to the grocery parking lot she was standing in. Occasionally coming in contact with someone's sneeze, though disgusting, had not heretofore been potentially deadly. All that changed with the virus. "The mask is there to protect others from you," PSA after PSA had said. How could such a simple thing cause so much anguish? For decades, signs had been posted on the doors of innumerable restaurants, bakeries, and stores: "No Shoes, No Shirt, No Service." Yet Marnie could not remember packs of screaming barefoot individuals outside the stores demanding to be let in. The mask issue had taken on a life of its own in this selfish, "me only" age, Marnie decided. If there was the slightest chance of being a carrier of a virus that is deadly to someone and you may not know you carry it, why not help out and just wear a mask? She was at a loss to explain when the world had become so thoughtless, so mean. Marnie thought back to social media posts she'd seen saying, "Let the old people die. If they are that fragile, they should stay home." She wondered if those writers ever thought about who would shop for the high-risk individuals who lived alone and had no one. Would *they* volunteer?

She made her way across the crosswalk and was nearly run down by a speeding SUV. "Why speed through a parking lot?" she thought. "Some child darting out from nowhere is going to be killed." She shook her head. Then she stepped through the front doors of the supermarket and into a hive of activity. The registers, the self-checkout lanes, and the store office were all busy trying to service the throngs of shoppers. She made her way cautiously toward the back of the store to the aisle with the canned vegetables. She was amazed as she passed bare shelf after bare shelf. The shelves that had previously carried every brand of toilet tissue, paper towel, or disinfectant of any kind were totally empty. Oddly, the section that held toilet bowl cleaner was completely stocked. Marnie thought, "Hmm, so no one cleans their toilets during a pandemic? Yuck."

She turned the corner to head for the potatoes. Down the aisle toward the end was a group of four young men. They laughed and talked with each other. Marine noticed that none of them was wearing a mask. She made an inconspicuous sound of disapproval, thinking, "You are carefree, healthy adults. I'm sure you couldn't be bothered with a mask." Then she heard what she thought was the staccato bark of a little dog coming from the group. Maybe a Yorkie? "I didn't think they allowed pets in the store," she thought. The sounds were in rapid succession. She was convinced it had to be a little dog until she heard two words.

"Bless you."

Marnie felt a chill run down her spine.

The accelerated spray had launched unseen from the mouth and nose of the shortest man in the group. No one had seen it because it was invisible. Each invisible particle, however, contained its own contingent of the virus. And each viral particle found a place on nearby surfaces to lie unseen until it could be transported to an unsuspecting host.

Marnie stopped short in the aisle. She had talked to her husband enough to know that she needed to wait a few minutes to let the particles settle. The laughter of the men continued as they moved to the next aisle. After waiting patiently, Marnie moved down the corridor to the canned vegetables. Carefully she picked up the can of yams with her fingers only, just in case the sneeze had contaminated the surface. She would certainly wipe that one down as soon as she got in the car. She always kept a packet of wipes in the glove compartment.

Each time Al returned from the store, he would call her and tell her he was in the garage. Then she would meet him at the door and take the grocery bags inside. There she would wipe all of the items down with disinfectant and let them sit for at least ninety minutes before putting the groceries away. But she didn't have time for that this morning because Lillian would be up soon. She would use more disinfectant and scrub harder. That'll do it, she thought.

Marnie mentally rehearsed all of the recommended safety protocols as she headed to the checkout stand. Weighing the differences in risk between facing an unmasked cashier and a finicky scanner, she decided on the self-checkout lane. After scanning her lone item, she placed it in the bagging area inside a store-supplied plastic bag. The metallic voice of the computer instructed, "Please remember to take your receipt and your change." She grabbed both, careful not to touch the machinery any more than absolutely necessary. Hurriedly, Marnie stuffed the receipt and the change into her large purse. She would wipe down the can and her hands once she got into the car so her steering wheel would not be an inadvertent carrier of the virus.

On her way out, Marnie saw an older man trying to take one of the two remaining shopping carts next to the big open doors of the supermarket but still inside the building. The carts were stuck together, locked in by the upturned flap that can be turned into a toddler seat. To dislodge the carts, he was using one hand to lift the flap and the other to pull the cart out. As Marnie approached, he yanked three times, but the cart did not come loose. The old man had put his cane under one arm, to free his hands, but trying to manage the cane and the carts was too much. Marnie approached him, and silently held up the baby seat flap, freeing the cart. He muttered, "Thank you, ma'am," and proceeded into the store. Marnie wondered how long he had been there and how many people had just walked past him. Her mind flashed back to the toilet paper hoarders. "Everyone get their own and don't worry about anyone else, huh?" she thought. When had the world turned so self-centered and cold?

Long before the pandemic, Marnie had seen the shift in the society around her. At the shopping center she had become used to seeing completely able people pull into handicapped parking spaces when the regular spaces were just a few feet away. At the cinema she often observed moviegoers deliberately leave coats on chairs so that no one could sit next to them even though seats were scarce, just because they wanted more personal space. Even her contemporaries laughed at her recycling efforts, not caring that their children would have to deal with the planet's environmental demise. There just seemed to be less compassion in the atmosphere.

Marnie turned and finally proceeded out the door, stepping onto the fluorescent-striped crosswalk. At that moment the slightest of warm Louisiana breezes picked up just to her left. It was the same type of breeze she remembered as a child when her mother would say, "Crack that window and let the breeze in." She quietly snickered, remembering her family's inside joke about a boy who was given the same command and innocently threw rocks that literally cracked the windows.

The slight breeze gently caressed her face. At that very moment the friendly breeze brought with it a tiny piece of dust. The dust found its way to the surface of the cornea of Marnie's eye. She blinked hard as she remembered not to touch her face. In blinking and shutting her eyes tightly just for a second she failed to see the truck approaching in her peripheral vision. The impatient driver blared his horn, startling Marnie as the speck of dust once again dug into the sensitive corneal tissues.

Disoriented, and startled by the horn, she reflexively wiped her right eye just enough to clear her vision as she quickly stepped out of the path of the supermarket "speedway" driver. It couldn't have been but a second, but a second was all it needed. The virus had found a home.

From the moment that thousands of viral particles landed on the can after being ejected from the nose and mouth of the sneezer, Q47cx knew its time was limited. It knew that unless it found a living host cell, it would die. Human hands could not save it because the tough outer layer of skin allowed it to be easily destroyed with soap or sanitizer. Once the can was wiped down, Q47cx would die instantaneously. It needed a warm living host cell. Suddenly its deliverance arrived. The soft, moist outer cells of the eye would provide a perfect home. As the virus settled in, its outer spike proteins deployed, attaching themselves to the cells. The invasion, and the takeover of each cell, had now begun. Q47cx would highjack Marnie's cells and make them its own private replication factories. It was the ultimate parasite; taking everything while contributing nothing. It owned her cells and would soon own her body.

12

THE FISHING TRIP ENDED LIKE MOST OF THEIR OTHER TRIPS.
Al and CC did not catch any fish worthy of Marnie's kitchen, and she
couldn't resist needling them just a little when they returned home. The
sound of the Jeep pulling into the driveway was her cue. "This is so
great," she said, walking out to the garage. "Another Saturday night fish
fry! Bring them right on in here, into the kitchen, boys, and I'll start
cleaning them." As usual, Al and CC good-naturedly defended themselves from Marnie's sarcasm before heading out back to relive the day's
events and have intense discussions about politics or sports.

Al and CC cherished their Saturday ritual. The few times they came back
with a fish or two, Marnie teased them that their haul was too small for
an entire meal before incorporating it into one of her recipes. Sometimes,
just to spare themselves from Marnie's teasing, they would stop by the fish
shack near the bayou and purchase a few catfish filets, already cleaned.
When they presented her with their alleged catch, they would playfully say
they had fished with "silver bait" that day. But the fish weren't important.
Al and CC treasured the time they spent together as friends.

After dinner, Marnie stuck to her usual routine, continuing preparations for Sunday dinner. She always did as much as possible on

Saturday so as to shorten the cooking time on Sunday. Sunday church services could run a little long, and if she did not start any preparations before three in the afternoon, they wouldn't eat until midnight. Often, during the seventy-fifth minute of the morning sermon, she would ask herself, "Ok, is there a reason we need to hear this again? You've said it four times already!" She would look at her watch and wonder why Baptist seminaries didn't teach that the human attention span is approximately three minutes per year of age, or that it peaks at about one hour, around a person's twentieth birthday. She had learned about it during her graduate coursework, when she'd had to study developmental pediatrics. Learning how long her little ones could concentrate had shaped her entire approach to lesson planning. It still surprised her how often clergy failed to take advantage of basic behavioral science. Toward the conclusion of the interminable sermon, she and many of the other congregants were already mentally preparing dinner, wondering about NFL games, or lamenting the lost time on the golf course. Marnie's Saturday night head start meant she and Al and could actually eat at a decent time on Sunday.

Humming contentedly and deftly moving around the kitchen, Marnie turned her attention to the sweet potato casserole. After carefully wiping down the can of yams, Marine ran it under hot water. It was necessary to remove every possibility of contamination. She dumped the large can into a rectangular Pyrex dish. The recipe actually called for fresh sweet potatoes, but she found that the already prepared yams could be ready in half the time. She didn't mind cheating a bit, especially because she knew that her cinnamon and pecan topping for the dish were famous throughout the neighborhood. Marnie was an experienced, intuitive cook who needed no recipes. She knew just how much butter, how much sugar, how much cinnamon, and how many marshmallows to use. By the time the oven had reached cooking temperature for about an hour, the aroma would start to seep out through the insulated doors. The heavenly scent would bring Al back into the kitchen begging for a sample that he *knew* would not be afforded him. At least not until Sunday. After being rebuffed, Al would rejoin CC out on the patio.

Marnie snapped all of the the fresh green beans and placed them into a large pot. Then she carefully distributed six or eight strips of bacon to give the beans flavor. The problem with green beans at most banquets and dinners she attended with Al was a horrid lack of flavor. They would giggle surreptitiously as they each left the crispy, tasteless green beans uneaten and noticed how many other guests did the same. In secret they referred to them as "white people green beans." They could never figure out why the cooks preparing the meals didn't just ask how to make green beans taste less like chewing tree bark. In another life Marnie would have been glad to show them.

Marnie was quite a culinary artist, but when her former school hosted potlucks or other such events, she always volunteered to bring something plain like rolls or store-purchased ham. She knew that if she brought a skillfully prepared dish to the event it would be enjoyed by all. But she also knew from bitter experience that later, after alcohol had loosened tongues and decreased inhibitions, someone would make a comment implying how well "you people" can cook, and the evening would be ruined for her. Since her second year of teaching, she always opted for a non-controversial path and usually brought Mrs. Shubert rolls.

One of her co-workers understood her reluctance to share her gift all too well. A science teacher at the high school level, Melvin Brown was also a gifted baritone. His velvety tone could melt hearts or shake rafters, and in his youth there had been whispers of a career on Broadway or at the Metropolitan Opera. But Melvin loved teaching above all else, and he and Marnie had become fast friends. Melvin was frequently asked to sing at school events but always graciously declined. The teaching staff did not understand why, but Marnie did. Not a word about it had passed between them, but she knew that if Mr. Brown sang at one of the functions, in his mind he would be reduced to the minstrel entertaining his superiors. It would only be a matter of time before someone would say, "Hey Melvin, give us a song" in one of the high-level meetings where professionalism was paramount. He and Marnie often discussed the need to keep their professional lives separate from their private undertakings. It was a chalk line that many African American professionals had to walk, and that was just the way it was.

"Need any help?" A bleary-eyed Lillian wandered into the kitchen. "It was a rough one last night," she said. "We lost three within a period of five hours."

"No," Marnie said. "Just sit here and keep me company."

Lillian went to the refrigerator and grabbed the last bottle of Mountain Dew, much to Marnie's disapproval. "It's just one, it's just one," Lil protested in a little girl's voice.

Marnie rolled her eyes and said, "Ok but that's the last one this week."

"Yes ma'am."

Both women laughed.

"Can you eat dinner with us tomorrow?"

"You know what? For once I'm not on call until the evening, so this weekend I can join you two," Lillian nodded.

Marnie looked up, surprised with a wide grin on her face.

Lillian began, as she usually did, by asking Marnie what she was making. Their conversation gently meandered from recipes to fashion to men to politics, all while Marnie's agile hands continued working and the Sunday dinner slowly took shape.

13

ON TUESDAY MORNING, MARNIE AWOKE WITH A LITTLE TICKLE in her throat. She coughed a couple of times but thought nothing of it. Maybe just some fall allergies trying to kick in. By noon the cough had increased, and now there was a burning sensation in her throat. She rationalized that it must have been the tacos she had for dinner Monday night. But by seven o'clock that evening it was clear the tacos were not the culprit. Marnie felt an intense burning in her throat, and she had a persistent cough and shortness of breath. Checking on his wife, Al kept asking, "Are you all right?"

"Sure, I'm ok, no problem."

Al was not convinced. He picked up the cell phone and punched in Lil Man's name. The call went straight to voicemail, but Lillian phoned back within fifteen minutes. She was on her first break and had gone to check her cell just in case there was a call. Her heart rate sped up slightly when she saw the professor's smiling face, his ringtone image, on her phone. She touched the answer tab and without saying hello asked, "Dr. McGuire? Is everything OK?" Doc had never called her when she was on duty. Not even once.

"I don't think so," a strained voice answered. "I think Marnie is sick. She says her throat is burning. She keeps coughing and she says she is short of breath."

Lillian felt a sudden shiver. "Dr. McGuire call 911 and get her to the hospital *now*," she said calmly.

"She won't want to go, you know."

"No, no get her here now. Hang up now and call 911."

Dr. McGuire obliged.

Lillian begged a fellow resident to cover her for just for an hour and she ran to the emergency department to meet the ambulance. In her soul she already knew it. She tried to come up with another explanation on her way to the emergency department, but M&M was not an asthmatic and had no known allergies as far as she knew. A simple cold would not give her the shortness of breath. Lillian continued down the list of potential differential diagnoses, but nothing fit the pattern. Sudden onset of shortness of breath and fever during a pandemic. Lillian knew, but couldn't yet admit it to herself. It was the virus.

A short time after Lillian and Al hung up, an ambulance sped up the McGuire driveway. The EMTs, dressed in full personal protective equipment, or PPE, made their way with Al's guidance to the bedroom. Marnie seemed even more short of breath than she had a couple of minutes before. Her breaths came in abrupt gasps, and her eyes could not hide the fear and apprehension provoked by the hunger for air. The EMTs rapidly placed an oxygen mask over her mouth and nose, turning the dial on the regulator to five liters. Some of the stress eased from Marnie's face but her quick gasps did not lengthen. The portable transport gurney had been lowered to bed height. Once she was strapped in, they lifted the level of the narrow bed to transport height and headed toward the door. While she was being loaded into the back of the vehicle, the third crew member, still speaking through a mask and shield, informed Al that he would not be able to ride with her to the hospital because regulations did not allow it. Nor should he should try to follow the ambulance because of the speeds it could reach with lights and siren. His best option was to drive to the hospital and meet them there.

Lillian waited near the ER door, prominently displaying her hospital ID so as not to be removed by the hospital security detail. Three transport vehicles rolled in and unloaded. No M&M. The fourth vehicle arrived, having cut the sirens upon entry to the parking lot. A PPE-clad attendant met the crew. Lillian heard "Seventy-five-year-old Black female in moderate respiratory distress. Gotta have iso." She knew "iso" referred to the isolation ward where suspected viral patients were kept. Her heart sank. They all knew. The experienced emergency transport staff knew. It was the virus.

Pulling on her own mask and face covering, Lillian made her way toward the gurney. "M&M, it's going to be OK," she said calmly, but Marnie did not answer. Talking just took too much effort. "Doc is on his way and I will see to it that he gets back here with you as soon as possible." She clasped Marnie's weakened hand and held it for a second.

"Gotta go, Dr. Manning," a female voice said to her.

Lillian released M&M's hand and said, "I'll be there in a minute." Then she scanned the parking lot and detected the form of a man with a slight limp nearly running toward the door. He was severely out of breath from his sprint. The unusually perceptive Lillian missed one small detail. She did not see the professor momentarily stop and squeeze his eyes together in a moment of pain. Looking the other way, she also missed the clenched fist the professor held in front of his chest. By the time she wheeled around to hand him a mask and a face shield left for hospital staff by the entry door, he had disguised his discomfort. He would tend to it later. For now, he had to get to Marnie.

"Put these on," Lillian said. "And don't say a word." Hospital security was heightened amid the viral outbreak, but she *had* to let Dr. McGuire see Marnie for what could be the very last time ... ever. The security guard had already seen and acknowledged her during her initial trip to the area, so she would fall under no further scrutiny. She unclipped her ID badge and handed it to Dr. McGuire. She said quietly, "When we turn the corner just hold up the badge." As they turned the corner, as soon as the guard looked up, Lillian said, "No, doctor, acyclovir and valacyclovir would likely not decrease the incidence of the cytokine overreaction."

The guard saw a doctor whom he knew to be a doctor. The man following her held up a badge and was being spoken to in what sounded like very scientific and medical jargon. The man must therefore be a doctor on the staff consulting with another doctor. It did not matter that the sentence Lillian uttered made no sense. It sounded complex, and the brain of the guard filled in the blanks. Lillian had known that his brain would, as long as it encountered a familiar enough pattern. Puzzles with upside down or missing words are still readable because the brain's job is to make sense of whatever it encounters. Lillian had just bet her career on it. She and Al slipped into the holding room uneventfully.

14

MARNIE'S BED POSITION WAS IN A CORNER, BEHIND A DRAWN curtain. There were three other occupied beds in the large room, but two puffy pink house socks with alligator eyes betrayed her location. This was a primary isolation room with less strict isolation. If her symptoms proved to match a rapid viral analysis, and she was positive for the virus, she would be moved to a maximum isolation ward where there was ironclad security. Al and Lillian made their way to her bedside.

"Talk fast, Doc. The bedside nurse could return any minute." Lillian moved aside to give the couple some privacy.

Dr. McGuire then stepped around the curtain and grabbed the hand of his college sweetheart. The words "talk fast" echoed in his brain. "I love you, Marnie. I love you; I love you" was all the oratorically gifted Matthew Seward Hagan Professor of molecular biology could muster. But after decades of marriage, that was all that was necessary.

Marnie's eyes answered with what her mouth struggled to utter, but he understood.

"Got to get her next door now, doctors," the young graduate nurse shyly said.

Yes, in the crisis, it was all medical hands on deck. Student nurses, graduate nurses and even medical students had all been issued various forms of battlefield commissions. It was wartime.

As Al and Lillian stepped away from Marnie's bedside, the professor could hide his physical pain no longer. This time Lillian noticed the professor take a small, flat tin from his pocket. Much too small to hold mints, she thought. Then she watched Dr. McGuire slip a tiny pill under his tongue. "Nitro?" she inquired.

"Yes," the older man reluctantly admitted.

"For how long?"

"About three years now."

There was no need to conceal the malady any longer—not from Lil Man anyway. The nitroglycerin tablet was medicine for his heart condition, angina pectoris.

Although not a heart attack, angina could cause a quite similar pain. A couple of years previously, Al had thought he was having a heart attack. He went to the emergency room on his own power and was evaluated. No markers of cardiac infarction were found, but he was diagnosed with angina. The ER doctor had explained to him that the vessels supplying blood to his heart were periodically spasming and decreasing blood flow to the heart muscle. Since the vessels were not totally blocked, a medication that allowed them to open would temporarily treat the condition. He was provided the nitroglycerin pills and instructed to follow up with a cardiologist. He never made the appointment, for two reasons. He was somehow able to get refills on the nitroglycerin by saying he had an appointment with the cardiologist, as he did not often need the pills. He only used them on the rare occasions he felt squeezing pains in his chest or when he had to climb the levees on fishing Saturdays.

The second reason he never met with a cardiologist was Marnie. He hated concealing things from her, but if she knew about his condition and the risk, she would spend every waking hour worried about him. It was likely that she wouldn't stop fussing over him, and doing things for him, and carrying his luggage, and telling CC not to take him fish-ing! Worst of all, she would change her sacred culinary creations into unseasoned turkey, salt-free flatbreads, and white folks' green beans! The professor had once heard an old doctor say, "Al, you can spend eighty years living or ninety years waiting for death." Al chose to take his eighty and a big bowl of Marnie's peach cobbler. Standing there in the isolation ward, Al couldn't believe he might never eat it again. Hands trembling, he slipped the tiny nitroglycerin tin back into his pocket.

15

DR. LILLIAN MANNING'S BORROWED HOUR WAS UP. SHE hurried back upstairs to resume her duties, but not before seeing Dr. McGuire to the exit. He mounted a protest but once a patient is admitted to the isolation ICU, no one, but no one, is allowed to remain with them. She promised to give him as many updates as she could. The conversation took a toll on Lillian because she knew what the possibilities were. That was one of the cruel things about this particular pandemic. Those on the outside, as yet unaffected, did not appreciate what a devastating toll the virus took after admission to the hospital. There was likely very little thought, by the young and low-risk individuals who held parties and drank at bars together, or who, with very cavalier carriage walked through grocery stores unmasked, that this could be their fate or the fate of someone they cared about.

These people did not care to know that once a patient is admitted to the emergency department, if they are suspected of having the virus, they are taken to an isolation room. They did not care to know that no one is allowed to enter the isolation room, so that the last time many family members see their loved one is at the entrance to the emergency department's isolation ward. Lillian's heart hurt when she thought of the decades that older couples had spent together, and that their very last contact would be a hurried glance at the entrance to an ER. She nearly broke down thinking of couples who had spent forty or fifty years together and maybe dreamed of their last sunset together, or of how one would hold the other's hand as the first peacefully transitioned. Instead they would say goodbye in haste and shock under cold fluorescent lights. At least Doc and M&M had avoided that cruel fate, but without her credentials, Lillian could have never gotten the professor in to see Marnie.

To make matters worse for infected patients, there was virtually no human contact with them at all. Even the medical staff, to protect their own lives, were clad in alien-like space suits with little ability to express a smile or a calming glance. There was no human touch, only the touch of cold vinyl gloves as intravenous lines were placed and secured. Though the virus seldom unleashed its wrath upon children, when it did, it was even more wrenching to witness. Lillian had seen one child hysterical from the time she woke up to the time she collapsed into sleep because no one whom she loved could be with her.

Lillian and her colleagues did have a few ways to spare patients some agony. When patients were placed on the ventilators for lifesaving breathing assistance, doctors could administer powerful sedative and paralytic medications to facilitate the process. They used a drug named ketamine to make the process go smoothly because it induces a trance-like state with sedation and memory loss. Once the ketamine was injected, the patient would not remember anything else until it wore off. Although Lillian knew that ketamine was a miracle drug that allowed patients to keep their sanity during incredibly invasive procedures, she also knew that the injection of the medication could be the very last thing a patient experiences on this planet. She often shuddered to think of it. If a patient did not recover from the devastating effects of the virus, then their final memory would be a ketamine injection. Recalling her religious upbringing, Lillian would think, "You go to sleep here and wake up in glory." The thought occasionally kept her up at night.

Realizing how lonely their experience could be when patients were not under sedation on a ventilator, the hospital chaplaincy came up with the idea of using electronic communication. Even though patients still could not be touched, doctors quickly recognized that communication with loved ones for a short time every day was amazingly therapeutic. Drives were held to collect money for the purchase of digital tablets, and many were donated to individuals who could not afford them. Escorting Dr. McGuire to the exit, Lillian had stressed to him that he needed to find Marnie's iPad, remove the cover, and bring it to the hospital. The instruction served the double purpose of enabling the couple to communicate and giving the professor a concrete task to help ease his anxiety. Lillian, during an incredibly busy night, only managed to contact Dr. McGuire once. The news was good, and the news was bad. Marnie had the virus but did not yet require a ventilator.

16

FOR AL, THE DRIVE HOME WAS EXCRUCIATING. HE WAS
driving away from a hospital where his Marnie remained. Who was
there with her? Was she afraid? Who would hold her hand? In many
ways the automobile was on autopilot. Al passed traffic lights without
really noticing whether they were red or green. Thankfully there were
no pedestrians out at that time of the evening. Most people were inside,
close to home. Al prayed the whole while he was driving. "Faith is an
easy thing to have, until you actually need it." Al remembered the words
of his very first pastor, heard in a small church where he sat nestled
between his parents, his short legs dangling over the edge of the pew.
He had not understood the meaning of that sentence for many years.
Slowly, as his life unfolded, he came to realize its truth. Arriving back at
the house, Al immediately began his two assignments.

During the check-in process at the hospital earlier that night, the
administrative clerk had asked whether Mrs. McGuire had a living
will. When Al replied in the affirmative, she asked that a copy of it be
brought to the hospital as soon as possible. Although it was customary
for each patient admitted to have a copy of the living will on file, the
standard procedure carried an increased urgency once the virus struck.

The hospital staff knew they would need written documents expressing their patients' wishes in order to accommodate a distressingly high number of life-or-death decisions. Al looked behind a closet door and found a small safe. The safe was similar to the ones found in hotel rooms except it had a manual dial instead of an electronic keyboard. Al turned the dials to the digits corresponding to Marnie's birthday, opened the door, and removed a large envelope.

Both living wills were in the same envelope. Their rationale had been that if something ever happened to them both at the same time, it would be easy for their families to find the appropriate documents. Al removed his and scanned the front page of the document underneath it belonging to Marigold McGuire. It was a standard boilerplate document stating the signatory's wishes and desires in case of prolonged hospitalizations or a final request for voluntary assisted dying. Except for the names, the two documents were almost identical. Al flipped the document closed and carried it into their home office to make a copy. While copying the final page, something caught his eye. Years before when the document was constructed, he and Marnie had discussed medical care. Each had decided that they did not wish to be placed on ventilators in the event of a terminal or chronic illness. Al froze for a full minute.

The fact that Marnie's illness could require a ventilator sent his mind racing. In an older woman, even an acute infection with little chance of recovery could be seen as a chronic or terminal illness. If she acutely deteriorated the doctors would have to abide by her own pre-stated desires and wishes to determine if she should be placed on the potentially life-saving machine. On the other hand, if she required a ventilator it would mean that her prognosis was very bleak indeed. Would she even want to be placed on one? The two of them had made those decisions with sound minds and faculties. Reversing one of the decisions now would be difficult if not impossible. He would just pray that it never came to that. He placed the copy of the living will inside another large envelope and laid it on the table by the door. It was ready for him to grab on his way out in the morning.

Embarking on his second task, Al began the search for Marnie's iPad. It wasn't in its usual spot on the nightstand. It wasn't in the kitchen or the laundry room. Al didn't bother to look in the car because of course Marnie had not been anywhere. He checked the cushions on the couch, knowing it was too large to be concealed there. He had to find the iPad. It would be his only way of having any chance of communicating with Marnie. He went into her dressing closet and looked around. Seeing the small room brought Al to tears. Deep and fearful tears. Anxious, relentless tears. There on the little wire rack perched on its own dedicated shelf was Marnie's "hair." Her prized possession that she never left home without. That the wig had been left at the house instead of riding with her to the hospital proved how serious her condition was.

On a short stool just in front of a vanity was a large purse. Al often teased Marnie about the size and weight of the purse. He would inquire about how many bricks she had inside. "Is this a one-brick trip or a two-brick trip?" he would tease. Not once had Marnie answered.

Just to be on the safe side, Al decided to check for the iPad in the purse. He opened the gold-crossed flap and peered inside. There, nestled inside three or four sales receipts, was the iPad. The green and yellow butterfly cover gave it away. Al removed it, pulling some of the receipts out with it. As they fell to the floor, he scooped them back up and carefully placed them back in the purse. A quick glance revealed an image of a little bear cub on one receipt with the slogan "Be Safe" held by the cub. It was the standard logo of Big Bear grocery market. Relieved to have found the iPad, Al placed it on the counter next to the living will. He knew he would not be allowed to stay long at the hospital the next day, but he would make sure to be there before first light.

There was no sleep for Al that night. He merely sat in his chair and stared at the place where Marnie should be. He turned the television on just for background noise but had no interest in anything on the screen.

He watched the clock constantly. It took a full hour for every minute to pass. If he left at five thirty, he would be at the hospital by six o'clock and would wait for Lillian to get off at seven. She would give him an update on Marnie's condition, and then he would give her the iPad and take the living will to the administrative office.

Lillian's words came back to him. "She doesn't need a ventilator, but she has the virus." She never left the house. Lillian was incredibly cautious. Al wasn't sick. How could Marnie have caught the virus? There must be some mistake. There had to be a mistake.

17

AL HAD ALWAYS BEEN FASCINATED BY THE BRAIN AND THE popular idea that we really only tap into ten percent of its capacity. He often mused that if we could tap into the brain's entire potential, we would destroy ourselves. We would telepathically fight wars of immense destruction and never leave home.

As a scientist who had made his life's work solving puzzles, Al knew that sometimes the eyes capture something that the brain does not process. The information is stored in the brain but is not processed or placed in context until minutes, hours or days later. Subconsciously something was bothering Al, but he could not put a finger on it. He recognized the feeling because it was the prelude to every scientific breakthrough he'd ever had. The nagging feeling that he'd missed something plagued him, but he couldn't figure it out. He slowly let it go and resumed staring at the clock.

When 6:00 a.m. arrived, he jumped up, ran some water on his face, and hurriedly brushed his teeth. He grabbed a bagel and some juice, practically inhaled them, and headed toward the hospital. There were a few more cars out than the night before, but the streets were still sparse. He carefully watched his speed because he had no inclination to deal with the police at that hour. Marnie had the virus? How? As careful as he had been there was no way she could have contracted it. There must be a mistake. Al sat for an hour with his eyes fixed on the exit door.

Lillian came through the door at 7:17. Obviously exhausted, she had a solemn look on her face. She scanned the parking lot for any sign of Dr. McGuire's SUV. He hit the horn with two short beeps, and she found his vehicle. The night had taken its toll. Lillian approached Dr. McGuire but kept her distance. No hugs for more than one reason. She wanted to hug her friend so badly but dared not to. No matter how many precautions she had taken, she still wanted to distance herself and never risk transmission of the virus.

"What is the latest?" the professor asked.

"She's about the same," came the distressed resident's reply. "She is on oxygen but still working pretty hard to breathe. Give me the iPad. I'll take you to the admissions desk for you to leave her paperwork."

Lillian walked the professor to the door informing the security detail that he had documents for the admissions desk but would not be going into any restricted areas. They passed without incident. They reached the desk and the professor waited his turn to be seen. When he was called, he sprang from his seat and stated that he had brought paperwork, a living will for Marigold McGuire, an ICU patient. Lillian indicated she would be right back and sped upstairs with the iPad. Al completed the work at the desk just as Lillian was returning empty-handed.

"Keep your phone with you at all times," she insisted. "When she calls there will not be much time to talk."

She led Al in the direction of his car as she moved toward the reserved parking area for doctors. He checked his phone to make sure it was fully charged. Then he turned the ringer up to full volume, selected "vibrate for all calls," and placed it in his upper shirt pocket. He would not miss a call from Marnie. No way. At 11:09 a.m., the phone chimed and vibrated. Jolted, Al realized he'd been sitting in the parking lot for nearly four hours and fatigue had overtaken him. The phone had startled him awake but he was instantly alert. Marnie!

Al could tell from the angle of the image that someone else was holding the iPad for Marnie. At first, she wasn't totally in the frame, but then the disembodied hand slightly moved the device so she could be seen. The old professor fought back the tears as he looked at Marnie and saw her as she'd been on the day of their wedding, his radiant bride. The otherworldly noises all around her distorted her voice, but it was still his Marnie.

She spoke in gasping tones. "I'm ok, Sweetheart. There are … some … leftovers from … Saturday in the … refrigerator."

"Marnie, Marnie, I'm fine. Don't worry about me. I just want you to rest and get better."

"I'm … sorry … you … have been up … all night." Her eyes drifted shut then were open again.

"I love you, Marnie," the professor choked out.

"I love you too," Marnie gasped.

A voice then said, "We have to hang up now."

"Talk later," whispered the professor. The screen went blank.

Al sat and thought for a long while. That was so Marnie. Barely able to breathe but worrying about his dinner. It wasn't a put on. It's just who she is, Al thought.

His mind stretched back to one December night thirty years before. Marnie had taken ill with food poisoning at an event. Al raced to get her, so they had to leave her car there until the next day. Marnie just kept apologizing for getting ill and causing everyone so much grief. She was an angel, his angel. Her selflessness is what made her the outstanding teacher she was. The children always came first. Now it was her turn to be cared for and she was still trying to look out for him. How could she be ill now? How could she have gotten the virus? There was just no way. No way at all.

18

THE NAGGING THOUGHT WOULD NOT GO AWAY. SOMETHING was bothering Al and he was having trouble pinpointing it. He always imagined himself to be somewhat of a supersleuth, like a few of his fictional heroes. Sherlock Holmes stories fascinated him. Listening to the old grainy radio programs as a child, he had tried to solve the mysteries before Sherlock, but never could. In later years he tried the same with television detectives like Columbo and Monk but again came up short. He finally decided that fiction writers had one up on him. They always knew who did it. In order to construct the plot, they had to know the ending. A distinct advantage when solving mysteries.

Al's mind went back to Marnie. He hated seeing her like that. He had spent his entire married life trying to make sure she wanted for nothing. She was in no way demanding, which made Al even more eager to get her anything he thought she wanted. He would have given anything to trade places with her right now. The street ahead of him was blocked. The yellow-vested road workers were pointing toward a detour as Al arrived. "Most likely a sinkhole," he thought. The detour placed him on an unfamiliar side street, but he could clearly see Mohican Thruway ahead. He would simply jaunt over, make the wider block, and get back onto his route home. The short stint on Mohican Thruway took him right past Big Bear Grocery. The smiling cub sat there with a sign placed in his hands that said, "Be Safe." Al saw the sign and started to sweat.

He arrived at home minutes later. The slow-rising automatic garage door was barely in position when he catapulted his SUV into its customary place. Seeing the sign had made the puzzle pieces fall into place. He ran to the bedroom and dumped the contents of Marnie's purse on the bed. He scrambled through all of the old receipts until he found it. There it was. The receipt from Big Bear Grocery. Al could not read the date on the receipt because it was blurred. He didn't have to. When the pandemic had hit full force, Big Bear Grocery had changed the logo electronically stamped on all of its receipts. Instead of just the smiling bear, they added the words "Be Safe" to each receipt. In Al's trembling hand he held a receipt with a smiling bear and the words "Be Safe" stamped onto it. Al allowed his eyes to trail down the slip to the only item purchased. One large can of yams. "No, no, no," he said aloud. "No, no." He could not contain his emotions any longer, and he wept.

19

MARNIE HAD GONE TO THE STORE. BUT WHEN? LIKE dominoes falling in reverse, Al's guilt tracked backwards. It had to have been during his last fishing trip with CC. If he'd never asked for sweet potato casserole, Marnie would be well now. If he'd never let CC talk him into going fishing, he would have been home and would have gone to the store himself. If he'd never been so crazy in his work, CC would not have had to force him onto the bayou to fish in the first place. The whole thing was his fault. He was responsible for Marnie's illness. Why, why, why did he ask for the wretched potatoes? It was all his fault.

Al's festering guilt could not be contained. His damaged psyche had to find a valve to release some of the self-loathing in order not to self-destruct. As much as he blamed himself for Marnie's illness, he was still plagued by one question. Why should a simple trip to a grocery store place someone's life in peril? Al went into the walk-in closet and looked for the skirt hanger where Marnie kept her mask. It was always there, but the hanger was empty now. If the mask wasn't there then she had worn it. The N95 would have protected her from almost any airborne pathogen. She must have had on the mask when she went to the store. The entire trip inside could not have taken more than fifteen minutes.

Ice began to form within Al's blood vessels. Marnie didn't inhale the virus. She had touched something.

Al's mind was now a maelstrom of irrational thoughts brought on by a torrent of anger, guilt, and remorse. He laid the receipts back onto the bed and walked out of the bedroom. He made his way down the ample hallway and turned to enter a seldom used guest bathroom. Opening a cabinet, he removed a box of sterile Q-tips. He walked back into the kitchen and laid them on the counter. From the second kitchen drawer he removed five plastic sandwich bags from their box. Placing them on the counter next to the Q-tips, he moved to the stove. Picking up the tea kettle and shaking it to make sure there was water inside, he turned on the gas stovetop. The bright blue flame came to life and he placed the kettle over it. Walking back into the garage he fumbled through the now rank garbage yet to be picked up. He found two empty cans. One of the cans had contained yams, while the other had held fruit cocktail. He remembered that Marnie had made Jell-O with fruit cocktail as a light dessert.

By the time Al returned to the kitchen, the kettle was starting to bubble but had not come to a full boil. A shrill whistle soon followed. Al took the first plastic bag, opened it, and for a very brief moment held it over the exiting steam. He quickly closed it, trapping some moisture inside. He repeated the process with each bag. Inside each bag he wanted moisture but not water. Carefully sealing each bag, he laid them on the counter. He opened the new box of sterile Q-tips, but before touching them he meticulously washed his hands and allowed them to air dry. Al removed one of the sterile Q-tips and placed it firmly against the inner crease of the top of the can that once held the fruit cocktail. In a circular motion he ran the swab around the entire perimeter avoiding the smoothly cut edge. He picked up the first bag and carefully place the Q-tip inside. He then sealed the bag.

After meticulously washing his hands again, he picked up a second Q-tip. He repeated the same procedure as before, this time around the edges of the can marked "Yams." Sealing the applicator inside the second bag, he took a permanent marker and marked "FC" on the first and "CY" on the second. Al repeated the process swabbing the cabinet door, the refrigerator door, and the steering wheel of Marnie's car. Each bag was labeled with the initials of the tested item or area. He carefully placed each bag in a nearly empty drawer beneath the cabinet and took a deep breath. Al returned to the den, sat in his chair, and stared at the blank television screen. At some point he drifted off into a light sleep. The vibrating of his phone startled him. It was 3:47 a.m.

Q47cx was shrewdly malevolent in its attack. The virus was aware that signals from its presence would stimulate the production of protective chemicals called cytokines. These cytokines would aid in the defense of its victim. Realizing this, Q47cx counterattacked by releasing an overwhelming excess of cytokines. Like too many soldiers stumbling over each other, the overproduction of cytokines produced an overpowering inflammatory response that would block vital physiological pathways, leading to the death of the target. The out-of-control immune system would kill its own host. Marnie was under attack.

She tried to stay calm, but Lillian's voice unwittingly conveyed the urgency. "Doc," she said, "I think you need to come to the hospital. There are some decisions we need to discuss." Lillian hated being dishonest with Dr. McGuire, but she could not tell him the whole truth and expect him to drive safely to the hospital. In fact, Marnie had gotten much worse. Her carbon dioxide level, which doctors measured to see how much of the used gas was leaving the body, was rising in her blood, and her oxygen levels were falling. She was drifting in and out of consciousness. In any other situation, a tube would be placed to assist her respiratory effort. In Marnie's case this could not be done. Her living will specifically included a "no ventilator" clause. She had been of sound mind and body when the will was constructed. Though Lillian petitioned for her colleagues to override that section, there were no legal grounds for them to do so. There was nothing they could do.

20

LILLIAN MET DR. MCGUIRE IN THE LOBBY OF THE HOSPITAL. There was no hiding it now. Marnie was in critical condition and time was of the essence. They raced up the elevator to the sixth floor where the ICU was housed. They stopped at the guarded hallway stand while she presented her credentials. "We have special permission for a video visit," she told the security guard, who allowed them to pass. She took Al along a second hallway to a quiet room outfitted with only a couch, a chair, and a small table bearing some flowers. A garden scene of Jesus with a lamb in His hands was painted on a mural.

"Do you have your phone?" Lil inquired gently.

Al took out his phone and turned it on.

She did the same, tapping in numbers at lightning speed. "This is Dr. Lillian Manning. I need 1602's nurse *now* ... Yes, I have him ... Can you get her the iPad?" Lillian twisted impatiently, shifting her weight from one foot to the next.

Al's phone made a strange noise, and the FaceTime call came in. It was Marnie. She was barely recognizable. Stunned by her deterioration over just a few hours, Al fought back the tears.

"Hi, Babe."

Marnie couldn't answer.

"I know it's hard to breathe, but they are going to have to put you on a ventilator and that will help."

Marnie managed the faintest of smiles as she almost imperceptibly shook her head.

Al thought of the will. "I will change the will. I will change that part. They have to put you on the ventilator."

Lillian started to cry, trying hard to stifle the sound. They both knew it wasn't only about the will. Even on a ventilator, Marnie had less than a 5 percent chance of surviving. Her age was a strike against her. Her previous history of cancer was another strike. Ventilators were now being rationed, though no one would speak openly of it. Lillian knew that an unwritten formula for ventilator allocation was secretly in place. Confidentially reviewed by the hospital ethics committee, a plan had been approved. Hospital administration understood that when those kinds of internal plans were reported in the media, institutions were usually vilified. Accusations of "playing God" and engaging in discriminatory practices were lobbed. But in fact, there was nothing new or unusual about the hospital's plan. Lillian was well aware that, on the world's battlefields, surgeons had to make such decisions on a regular basis. Resources could not be used on a soldier with little or no chance of survival while another soldier with much better prospects died. Even if Marnie could be ventilated, she would have to line up behind thirty-five- and forty-year-olds who had a much higher probability of surviving.

Al got hysterically louder. "The ventilator!" He turned to Lillian, shaking his head and repeating "The ventilator! The ventilator!"

Lillian could hold back no longer. Despite social distancing requirements, she put her arms around the older man and shook with sobs.

Turning his attention back to his phone, Al said, "Marnie we are going to put you on the ventilator. We are! We are!"

Marnie's eyes drifted closed and fluttered. She struggled to open them and mouthed the words with no sound, "I love you."

"No! no!" the professor shouted. "This isn't right. This is not how it ends … I can't even hold her. I can't hold her hand … Marnie, Marnie … no, no, no … We are going to get a ventilator," his words trailing off into sobs.

With her final ounce of strength, Marnie smiled, looked directly at the screen, and silently, with a tiny smile, mouthed the word "Decaf." Then she closed her eyes.

21

LILLIAN HAD WITNESSED IT SO MANY TIMES IN THE MONTHS before Marnie's illness. The virus not only robbed each family of a life but also pillaged the dignity of the victim's death. Following a fatality caused by the virus, funeral homes were contacted and had to act immediately. Bodies were double shrouded and labeled. Full personal protective gear was worn by each funeral home employee in the vicinity of the deceased. There was no warm, compassionate planning, individualized for each family. Hastily formed regional guidelines were dropped into place, in a process that seemed more suited to factories than funeral homes. There was no public viewing and no open casket. Closed casket memorials were limited to gravesites with ten or fewer family members standing at least six feet apart. How could a family decide which ten members would attend when so many relatives were close to the deceased? The ensuing conflicts ravaged family ties already crippled by mourning.

Things were no different in Marnie's case. The impersonal transfer of her body to the funeral home, the business-like call to discuss "disposition of the body," and the fact that there would be no real homegoing service added to the crushing, numbing grief.

I sometimes hold it half a sin
To put in words the grief I feel;
For words, like nature, half reveal
And half conceal the soul within.
　　　　　—ALFRED LORD TENNYSON

Such was Al's grief, expressed by a favorite poet of his. Whatever amount of pain, however many tears, whatever grief Al showed was a mere fraction of what he actually felt. In his own mind, he likened his pain to being wrapped in a blanket full of broken glass. Whether he sat or lay down, stood or moved, the pain was equal on all sides. Lillian was not much better as she carried both the burden of M&M's loss and the pain of watching Doc drown in heartache.

The service at the graveside was very short and very personal. The small party consisted only of Al, Lillian, and CC and his wife. An associate minister from the church they occasionally attended delivered the eulogy. The young man did not really know Marnie, so his remarks were generic. Their elderly senior pastor was sheltered in place and had not left his home in many weeks. Al thought of the hundreds of people who would have been there to wish their beloved Mrs. McGuire good travels if they had been allowed. The students she touched through the years were innumerable. Of course, there were those who thought she was the reincarnation of Lucifer, but they were few in number. They were the students who earned poor grades because they did not try. Marnie was like that. If a student poured effort into their work, they were rewarded, maybe not with an A, but they knew their efforts had been appreciated. Marnie firmly believed there was nothing more loathsome than a smart kid who didn't care. That's the kind of teacher she was. How tragic that, of all things, the carelessness she despised had killed her.

The usual formalities—selecting clothes for the viewing, arranging a manicure, applying pancake makeup to hide the evidence of illness—had not been necessary. There was no viewing. When Al had returned home immediately following Marnie's death he had gone straight to her dressing closet. Looking at her clothes, he had wondered what he would have chosen under different circumstances. On one thing he would not compromise. He had carefully removed Marnie's wig from its little stand and placed it in a box. He had driven to the funeral home and encountered an attendant at the door. Tearfully, he had explained that Marnie must be interred with her wig and that it had to be placed on her head just right. Some attendants would have flatly informed him that the sealed casket could not be opened, but serendipity had placed him at the door just as one of the more experienced employees was on duty.

The kindly attendant knew that the casket would not be opened. It was sealed for good. But she had looked at the grief-stricken older man and said, "I will personally make sure it is placed on Mrs. McGuire exactly as you say." To further reassure Al, she had asked, "Did you say you need a little part right here?" The churchgoing attendant was well aware that commandment number nine is "Thou shalt not bear false witness against thy neighbor" and that most people interpreted it to mean "Thou shall not lie." But she felt no remorse about the untrue statement she had told this man. She had witnessed and honored her neighbor's grief. Somehow, she felt that God would forgive her.

Arriving home from the gravesite, Al felt completely alone. Lillian stayed at the house as long as she could, but she had a grueling shift awaiting her and had to get back to the hospital. Lil was the closest thing to a daughter he had ever had. Lillian felt the same way about the professor. For all intents and purposes, he was her father. She worried that he would actually waste away, knowing that inseparable couples frequently pass away within days or weeks of each other, even with no related illnesses. The survivor's will to live fades; the spouse left behind gently departs, to join the one who is deceased. But Lillian did not yet know that Al would not give up so easily. She did not know of his steely conviction that before he left this earth, he had to solve the puzzle of Marnie's death. He would not, *could* not leave it unfinished. He walked to the table and picked up Marnie's iPad.

22

UNSURE WHETHER HE REMEMBERED THE CODE TO THE IPAD, Al took his best guess. At every hotel that housed a safe in the room, Marnie always used the same code. It was her date of birth. Al typed in the code and the iPad powered up. He touched the icon for pictures and a cascade of photos glided across the screen. The very first photo in the gallery was of him and Marnie on a cruise. It had been taken quite a few years previous, and Al remembered neither the name nor destination of the ship. He only remembered eating six times a day and playing slot machines. He remembered the fun of losing quarters in the machine, smiling as each coin fell into the abyss. On one of those mornings, about two thirty, he had felt a tap on his shoulder. He'd turned to see a stern-faced Marnie standing beside him. "Do you know what time it is?" she had scolded. "Yep," he had said. "It's vacation time." Marnie had turned and gone back to the cabin. Al had slept through breakfast the following morning.

The days after the funeral were spent much like that first night. Al paged through memory after memory in his mind, often spontaneously smiling when a new one came forward. Yet the memories took their toll. Al lost weight as he ate very little. Lillian would frequently bring carryout meals for him and leave them in the refrigerator. But often, when she arrived with a meal, she would see that the previous one had not been touched. Al was falling into a deep depression but deceived himself into believing that it was just normal grief. He began to talk to Marnie late in the evening hours, actually having conversations as though she were responding to him. Lillian heard one of those one-sided conversations one evening and quietly wept in her room.

Each time Al visited a public place, his depressive grief turned to white-hot anger. The unmasked throngs had killed his Marnie. He watched as happy young people, mostly men, strolled around, spewing their pestilence in all directions. How could they laugh? Didn't they know Marnie was dead? It was a simple mask! No great sacrifice there. Just a small face covering worn for a few minutes in places where old people were required to go, just to help them stay healthy, stay alive. In his mind all those maskless people were complicit in Marnie's death, and he hated them. He would leave a store, often without having purchased anything, always in a rage. A store is where she had to have caught the virus. It couldn't have been anywhere else. They all needed to pay. They all needed to feel what he was feeling. They had callously placed their own temporary discomfort above Marnie's life. The hateful musings Al saw on social media platforms seemed even more vile now. It was a mask. Not sulfuric acid to the face. A mask!

How could old people "just stay home"? Would the anti-maskers be willing to shop for them? Would they be willing to come by twice a week and see that they had enough toiletries and household items? No, they were too busy hoarding pickup trucks full of toilet tissue and hand sanitizer to stock their closets while ignoring the fact that others couldn't even cover their basic needs. From what circle of hell had this species arrived? He had to get back to the car and tell Marnie to stay out of there. He had to protect her. But when he got to the car, she wasn't there.

The sliver of rational thought Professor McGuire had left was being devoured by the rage inside his head. Reason hung on by asking, "What if her infection wasn't even related to the store? What if it was the mail, in or on some delivered package? What if Lil Man, despite her meticulous decontamination routine, had missed a spot and infected Marnie?" There was only one way to find peace. He had to know. He had to know for sure. Professor McGuire returned home and went into his kitchen. He announced his arrival as he had for decades. "I'm home, Dear!" That no answer came from the empty house seemed not to bother him. He went straight to the kitchen. He opened a drawer and took out the five plastic sandwich bags he'd stored there earlier. Each bag contained a single cotton-tipped swab. He laid them on the kitchen counter and made a call.

23

DR. BELINDA TORRES WAS JUST FINISHING UP HER DAY WHEN the call came in.

"Bee, its Al McGuire, how are you?"

"Al! How are you my friend?" With a slight Puerto Rican accent, her voice registered both pleasure and surprise. "I was so sorry to hear about your wife. I only met her once, but she seemed to be such a wonderful lady."

"She is," replied Al. "She really is." It had been weeks, but Al refused to speak of Marnie in the past tense.

Dr. Torres noticed and felt a twinge of concern for her old friend. After a slight pause she regained her composure and asked, "¿Qué te trae a mi puerta?" Dr. Torres was not sure her old acquaintance remembered any of the Spanish she had taught him during their time working together, but the question seemed to lighten his mood.

He paused for a minute before haltingly responding, "Necesito un pequeño favor … and that's as far as I can get in Spanish."

They both laughed, and Al suddenly realized that he had not laughed in weeks.

Dr. Torres was a world-renowned virologist. Her work developing sequencing algorithms for viral identification was legendary, but only in the scientific community. When it came to public acclaim, her colleagues were always the ones to be rewarded. She and Al shared a bond in that way. They had gotten to know each other when they'd worked together at an institute one summer. The institute's fellowships were sponsored by a scientific think tank, and places were granted by invitation only. Experts from both industry and academia were invited to present research and share cutting-edge theories for two weeks. Seated at the same luncheon table for one session, the two scientists had started a conversation. In a short time, they realized they had a lot in common. Both should have been department chairs but neither were. At the end of that luncheon where they figured out that they had both been subject to the same indignities, they dubbed the meal The Passed-over Meal. They kept that joke to themselves.

"You know my Marnie died of complications to the virus. I'm just trying to do some transmission testing. I know the major mechanism of spread is airborne, but I want to detect some possible levels of contamination that may not be airborne. So I just want you to test a few samples for me, run some PCRs on them, and see what you find. I could probably ask one of the guys here, but you know how they're always prying. If I come up with a discovery, I want it to be dedicated to Marnie's memory in the paper I write. I am specifically looking for viral fragments of the Q47cx virus. Beyond whether it is there, I want to know, if you find it, whether it's the same in each sample."

Dr. Torres was one of the original pioneers of polymerase chain reaction, or PCR, in which a tiny fragment of the genetic material is duplicated millions or billions of times for easier identification and study.

"You got it my friend. Send me the samples."

Forty-eight hours after their phone conversation, a FedEx truck delivered a package containing five plastic bags containing cotton-tipped applicators to Dr. Torres's lab. Late for a meeting, she placed them in her private office and vowed to work on them the following morning. The work was completed in six days. When she finished, she compiled a short list of her findings and wrote them in an email to Dr. McGuire. She phoned him to let him know that his results were on the way.

"By the way, what mechanisms of spread are you looking into?"

"Well, I'm trying to figure out from a quantitative standpoint how much time is needed for tactile transmission of the virus," he lied. "I think if I can come up with some time frames it may help schools know how to safely distance and reopen. Just trying to keep busy in my free time."

"That's admirable," she replied. "Look for that email from me. I hope it will help. Oh and I did exactly as you asked. When I found viral particles present, I compared them to see whether they originated from the same source. They did." She hung up. A minute later Al's phone beeped. He had an email.

WITH THE VIRUS SHOWING NO SIGNS OF SLOWING ITS DEADLY
spread, Lillian had little time to check on Dr. McGuire. She knew he was
taking Marnie's death exceptionally hard and seemed to spend most of
his time in his laboratory at the school. She hoped they weren't true, but
she was hearing rumors that the once brilliant scientist was slowly going
crazy. People whispered to each other that he could often be seen carrying on conversations as the only occupant of his car. Lillian rationalized
that hands-free cellphones had been available for years, but she knew deep
down that the professor likely did not know how to enable his Bluetooth.
Her misgivings about his mental health came into focus when, on one of
her rare nights off, she and a friend went to dinner.

When Lillian entered the restaurant, she noticed a man sitting alone
in a darkened corner. Dr. McGuire. Lillian was elated that the professor
had finally decided to get out of the house and have dinner elsewhere.
She started to approach his table but stopped short when she saw there
were two menus placed on the table. She assumed he would soon be
joined by a friend and did not want to bother him. As the evening wore
on Lillian and her friend, a former resident in her training program,
finished their meal. But no one had yet joined Dr. McGuire. Curious,

Lillian asked her server how long the restaurant usually holds a table for two if only one has shown up. The server followed her gaze and volunteered, "Oh, that guy. He's here at least twice a week, and no one ever shows up. He requests a table for two, gets two menus, orders his drink and a glass of water, and two entrees. He eats his food and leaves the other entree. No one ever comes. No one bothers him because he is a very generous tipper. We don't know his name. We just call him Crazy Fred." Fighting tears, Lillian asked for the check.

At approximately nine thirty, Lillian dropped her friend at her door and headed for her "apartment." Now it was clear why she saw so little of the professor at home. His brilliant analytical mind refused to accept Marnie's death. He still talked with her and took her to dinner as though she had never left. Psychologically keeping his wife in suspended animation allowed him to function, and he had never accepted the fact that Marnie was truly gone. In his mind she would always be there.

Lillian couldn't help but think about how genius and mental illness are frequently associated with each other. She thought of all the "mad scientist" characters she'd encountered in science fiction films and spy thrillers. She didn't know it, but Al had actually been having similar thoughts. He had even questioned his own sanity. Then he had considered his methodical investigation into Marnie's death and reasoned that true creative thought, like the kind research demanded, cannot exist alongside wild swings in emotion or distorted reality. Though he was slipping into a deep depression, Dr. Alton McGuire was confident that he was not psychotic. He simply had a laser focus that sometimes did not allow him to fully consider, or accept, the realities of everyday life. He had experienced that kind of focus only a few other times in his entire life, most often when working on his research. In such a state, he was utterly unaffected by the thoughts of those who might find him strange or eccentric. His only priority at the present moment was fully exploring the circumstances of the events that ended not just his wife's life, but his as well.

25

AL CLICKED ON THE ICON FOR HIS EMAIL AND HIS INBOX CAME
to life. Quickly deleting the top three emails, he arrived at the one sent
by Dr. Torres. The email dispensed with perfunctory platitudes and
went straight to the results of her evaluation. Thinking that each pair
of initials was code for a particular patient, she had been careful not to
make any mislabeling mistakes with the samples. Her results read:

FC: No viral particles
RD: No viral particles
SW: Moderate viral particles
CD: No viral particles
CY: Numerous viral particles

Al stared at the email a very long time. He remembered a television
commercial he had seen many years before, an ad for a glass repair company. The ad opened with the photograph of a beautiful house with
a large picture window. An errant throw from a nearby yard landed
a baseball right into its center. The glass shattered into thousands of
pieces. The voiceover artist then said, "Let Econoglass put your picture

back in focus." At that point the frames were played in reverse and the glass suddenly sprang back into place, each of the thousands of glass shards miraculously falling into perfect position.

In Al's mind, the final puzzle of Marnie's infection and death had just come into focus.

For weeks he had wondered how Marnie could have contracted the virus. Finding the receipt from the store had given him a theory, but there had been no proof. Dr. Torres's report made it all plain. FC: There had been no viral particles on the fruit cocktail can. Marnie would have prepared the meal like she always did, placing all of the things she needed on the counter before she began. That was her organizational method. The fruit cocktail can had stood there, but she had not transmitted any virus to it. Her hands had been clean when she touched it.

RD showed no particles. That was the swab taken from the refrigerator door handle. Therefore there had been no viral particles on her hands when she handled the door. SW had moderate viral particles. That was the sample taken from her steering wheel. At some point while in her car she'd had viral particles on her hands. But once she had entered the house, those particles had been eliminated by her meticulous hand washing. She always sanitized her hands and wiped down cans as soon as she arrived home, so the transfer had undoubtedly occurred before then.

The cabinet door, CD also showed no viral particles. That result confirmed that Marnie had followed her routine and thoroughly washed her hands before any preparation of food. The CY, however, was a different story. It was loaded with viral particles. The particles were the same as the ones found in lesser quantities on the steering wheel. A clear picture emerged.

Marnie had gone to the store unbeknownst to either Lillian or himself. At some point in the store she picked up a can of candied yams, which the sales receipt verified. There had to have been some type of contamination that occurred during the time frame between when she touched the can and when she got home. By the time she had reached the house and washed her hands, the inoculation of the deadly virus had already occurred. She had been masked. Had she had the virus before her shopping trip, she could not have transmitted it in such great quantities to only the candied yams and nothing else. That the can was contaminated when she touched it was the only conclusion. Since the virus has a limited life on surfaces, a large amount had to be applied to the can just a short time before she picked it up. There had been enough virus on the can so that Dr. Torres had detected numerous particles even after Marnie had wiped it down. The possibility of shedding enough virus to blanket a can while wearing a face covering was remote. Even if some small amount of virus had escaped a cloth mask, it would not have been enough to spread disease except in a vanishingly small number of cases. There was no other conclusion. The virus that had infected Marnie had very likely been spread by one of the unmasked, possibly an asymptomatic or pre-symptomatic carrier.

Al surmised that the culprit was young. An older person, by the time they had enough of a viral load to easily spread disease, would have probably been symptomatic, weak, and unlikely to be shopping on a Saturday. Whenever he had observed couples, Al had noticed that young women often wore face coverings but their accompanying significant others often did not. These macho men could not be bothered with wearing a mask to protect someone else's life. Science is often a game of probability, and Al was reasonably certain that he could accurately describe the culprit responsible for Marnie's death: a young adult male, unmasked in the midst of a global pandemic.

26

PROFESSOR ALTON McGUIRE WAS AWAKENED BY HIS OWN screams. He sat bolt upright in his bed, where he only rarely slept, drenched in sweat. The dream had been all too real. Willing himself to return to the present, he sat in bed and methodically replayed what he had just experienced. The experience had not felt at all like a dream. It had been too real, too vivid. The squeezing pain in his chest intensified. He fumbled for the small tin of medication in his top bedside drawer. He removed one of the nitroglycerin pills and placed it under his tongue. The pain gradually subsided. He slowly began to relive the nightmare.

He was looking into a classroom window. Marnie stood in front of a little boy of eight or nine. There was a lesson of some kind going on, as she was writing on the chalkboard. She wrote a few sentences with her back to the boy. When she turned around the boy had grown into a young man. He seemed engrossed in the lesson as Marnie continued to teach. She wrote another group of sentences on the board, turning her back to the young man. At the conclusion of the lesson, the young man smiled and handed Marnie a picture he had drawn. The picture showed a beautiful bayou scene with the sun rising in the early morning. As Marnie held the picture, out of the bayou on the picture rose the head of a snake. Opening its mouth, it was the unmistakable pale color of a cottonmouth. Marnie tried to drop the book, but it would not leave her hands. She shook her arm furiously as the viper continued to emerge. She screamed for Al. Al picked up a rock to smash the window pane, but the rock turned to sand in his hand. He screamed her name as the snake coiled. More and more frantically Al screamed and tried to get into the classroom. The whole thing unfolded in slow motion. He tried to smash the glass with his hands to no avail. The large snake coiled and struck Marnie's neck. It attached itself as the deadly venom poured inside her spasming body. As Marnie fell to the floor, the creature slithered away. Al was left screaming, "Marnie, Marnie!" Her eyes slowly closed. In his mind, even in the dream, Al was transported to the banks of a bayou many years before. The cottonmouth. The snake that had tried to kill his grandfather. That monster had not escaped the crosshairs of Al's singular focus, a focus that made the outside world disappear. But this time, he had not killed the monster in time. He had failed to save the one he loved.

Fully awake now, Al collected his thoughts. In his dream he had failed. Retribution was now his only recourse. The monster responsible for Marnie's death was a young man. An arrogant, self-absorbed, entitled young man had killed his beloved. Suddenly the logical part of his brain began to reassert itself, and Al realized that there was no way to determine whose toxic venom had been placed on a can that ultimately killed his Marnie. His rational mind knew that he had to let it go. He had investigated and found the source, but that was as far as he could go. He wrestled with his thoughts for the remainder of the night, but by morning he knew he had to make a decision, to even be able to live from day to day. His existence at present could not be called living.

Throughout the morning, images from his dream returned to Al again and again, and he racked his brain for every piece of information about dreams he had ever encountered. He had never before had a dream that felt so lifelike, that had chased him across the boundaries of consciousness. He could not shake the feeling that it had to mean something. Suddenly he had a memory from his first year of marriage. Late one night he had been watching Marnie sleep, as he often did, and when she awoke, he teased her that he'd seen her dreaming.

"How do you know I was dreaming?"

"Well Miss Jackson," Al flirted, "I saw your eyes moving rapidly from side to side, and your eyelids were fluttering, so I know you were in REM sleep. And that's the stage of sleep in which most dreaming occurs."

Marnie rolled her eyes. "Always an answer for everything. Come here, Mr. Know-It-All." She pulled him into her embrace, and they both slept peacefully through the night.

There was no way to ever find the young man who had cost his wonderful Marnie her life. Maybe it wasn't a man at all. Maybe it was a woman or a child. No, the dream had specifically shown a young man. Al stopped himself. Was he, a man who had devoted his life to the scientific method, really looking for clues in a dream? He shook himself and tried to reason. On the one hand, he thought, psychologists considered dreams to be an expression of subconscious thought. And physiologists had established that during REM sleep the body makes chemicals to relax and even paralyze muscles so that people don't unwittingly act out their dreams. All of that argued for a clear boundary between reality and sleep. On top of that, Al knew that sleep deprivation causes REM sleep to increase, so someone getting too little sleep, like he was at the moment, might well be expected to have more vivid dreams. But on the other hand, Al knew he'd been even *more* sleep deprived as a graduate student and young professor, sometimes going forty-eight or seventy-two hours without rest, and he had never had such a dream. He also knew that around 95 percent of dreams are forgotten immediately upon awakening. Those facts seemed to argue that his dream was real.

It had to be real. He thought about Joseph, whose childhood dreams predicted his rise in Egypt as Pharaoh's right hand man. The Bible was full of God directing the actions of men through dreams. And hadn't

Abraham Lincoln dreamt of his own assassination three days prior? Al's mania gathered momentum as he remembered that Niels Bohr's model of the atom had been revealed to him in a dream and that Einstein's theory of relativity had its roots in a childhood dream. Those examples proved that scientists should pay attention to dreams, that it wasn't all just paranormal nonsense. Al's dream had been so vivid and kaleidoscopic that he became convinced it was a message.

But the dream had not revealed any facial features. There had been no identifying features at all. There was no way Al could single out Marnie's murderer and exact his revenge. He had to abandon hope of ever finding one young man among thousands. He could stand in Big Bear Grocery all day but would not be able to tell who, on that day, had been the careless one. Al slumped his shoulders, wiped his face with his hand, and came to a chilling realization. He would just have to kill them all.

27

AL KNEW THAT THE OVER-MASCULINIZED, TESTOSTERONE-filled, fictional scripts of Hollywood were fantasies and that, in almost every way, women were the stronger sex. For decades it had been common knowledge in the scientific and medical communities that women fare much better in response to infections than men do. Al thought back to an article by a Belgian scientist that he had read many years before. Dr. Claude Libert and his associates had observed that females are better able to recover from episodes of shock brought on by sepsis, infection, and trauma. Al also recalled that females of many mammalian species live longer than males, and in general enjoy better health. Nodding to himself, Al thought of the large numbers of widows residing in the sunbathed communities of Florida.

Dr. Libert's team proposed that biological mechanisms of the X chromosome have a strong impact on an individual's genes, which gives an immunologic advantage to females. They postulated that males are at a disadvantage because they have only one X chromosome. Other research Al had read theorized that females of the species evolved to be more immunologically competent because immunity must be conferred to unborn offspring. Contemporary literature bore this out, as did preliminary data from the current pandemic. Equal numbers of women and men contracted the virus, but far fewer women died from infection. That genetic superiority was not lost on Al.

Yes, he had to kill them all. The plan to devastate the young male population was taking shape in Al's mind. He would not target older men and also hoped that they would be more likely to take precautions and adhere to public health guidelines. Even though he knew some of them would not, he resigned himself to the fact that in every battle there must be collateral damage. He hated the idea, but it was unavoidable. There was nothing he could do about it. The young men must die in great numbers. Marnie's killer would be among them. That is all that mattered.

Al had watched enough murder mysteries to know that the most successful plots are executed in the midst of chaos. When a murder took place in the middle of a housefire, or a homicide happened during a hurricane, the investigations were much more difficult. That's the model he would use. A sudden upswing in infection rates of a deadly virus would raise no suspicion. Those who investigated such matters would surely attribute the deaths to a spontaneous mutation of the virus. It was the perfect cover. The professor had two objectives to carry out. First, he had to chemically alter the virus to become much deadlier. He would accomplish that task by causing a drift in the properties of the virus, partly by increasing the number of spike proteins on the surface of each viral particle. The spike proteins would allow the virus to attach much more tightly to the host cell, thus inflicting greater damage.

Next, he had to somehow lower resistance to the virus of a particular segment of the population: men. This second task was partially taken care of, as males were already more susceptible to the most lethal effects of the virus. He just had to find a way to exploit that fact. To carry out his two-pronged plan, he would need to spend more time in his laboratory at the university. As an emeritus professor, it had been some time since he had spent an extended amount of time there, so he needed a plausible cover so as not to attract attention. Not only would he need an explanation for his presence but he would also need to gain the trust of working colleagues by purporting a noble cause.

He decided to pen a letter to the chairman of the molecular biology department at the university.

Dear Professor Steichen:

Let me first commend you on the brilliant research continuing to pour forth from the cutting-edge researchers in your department. The most recent paper on the mapping of internal proteins in novel RNA viruses was ingenious. Reading it stoked the fires of curiosity that burned so bright during my years at the institution.

As you are no doubt aware, a few months ago I lost my wife of forty-three years to the effects of the Q47cx virus. It is my intention to resume some of the work in the laboratory so generously afforded me by the university. This letter is merely to let you know, and to let the other faculty and staff know, that they should expect to see me there at least a couple of times a week. Although you were not in your present position through most of my academic career, you may have heard of my idiosyncratic habit of working late at night. This allows me to remain out of the way of other, more energetic young minds.

It has been stated that through tragedy inspiration is often born. I intend to focus my work on how we may diminish the effects of mutating viruses in the future. As I have no need to publish any findings, should I arrive at a particularly interesting discovery, I will simply turn my work over to one of your capable faculty members and allow them to proceed how they see fit. Consider me just to be an able assistant.

Once again, I would like to thank the university for allowing me to continue in some capacity as we search for answers of some of our most challenging problems.

Sincerely,

Alton McGuire, PhD, Professor Emeritus

Al was sure the letter would bring a silent chuckle from the arrogant Dr. Steichen. He would consider Al to be just another dawdling old fool playing with test tubes in a make-believe lab. What harm could there be?

28

LILLIAN NEARLY HAD THE HOUSE TO HERSELF NOW. SHE didn't mind it very much, although she sometimes missed laughing and talking with Dr. McGuire. Marnie's death had made the arrangement somewhat awkward, and she had offered to move out. She was amazed at how quickly small-minded people could change their opinions about a situation. Practically everyone knew that the three of them had been like a family when Marnie was alive. Lillian was the daughter the McGuires had never had. She was often there when friends visited. Her little space was detached and practically separate from the main living areas. Still, after Marnie's passing there were those who whispered about the young physician living out there with the professor. Lillian was amazed at how small and cruel people could be.

It wasn't just the living quarters that kept Lillian at the Tudor. She was genuinely worried about Dr. McGuire. She had decreased the amount of meals she purchased and left in the fridge because he rarely ate at home. She couldn't really verify her worries because she barely even saw him. Maybe he was doing just fine, and they just each had their separate agendas. She had no way of knowing. Most of the time Lillian was home, she just slept. She had no social life. As a physician at the heart of the pandemic, she knew the most important thing she could do was to stay sharp and get all the rest she could. The red "racecar," her pride and joy, had become little more than a commuting taxi as her weekend stints at the go-kart track and her backroads excursions took a backseat to the unfolding crisis.

Her mind drifted back to the dinners the three of them had once shared, and the joy Marnie took in preparing them. She missed the kitchen table talks with the woman who had mothered her just as if she'd given birth to her. She fondly remembered the last meal they had eaten just before Marnie became ill. It still troubled her greatly, the question of how Marnie had become infected. At times her rational mind was forced to step in to overrule her guilt. There was simply no way she could have infected Marnie. Her ritual was too careful, too meticulous, too grooved into her muscle memory. Shortly after Marnie's hospitalization, Al had wondered aloud morning, noon, and night where and how she could have become infected. It dawned on Lillian that, oddly, Dr. McGuire never seemed to ask those questions anymore. She guessed that he had just resigned himself to the fact that he would never know.

As Lillian sat, half-dressed on the side of her bed, her thoughts were interrupted by Beyoncé singing "Single Ladies." That was the ringtone she had installed specifically for Dr. McGuire. In a split second, she traveled back in time to the moment she had chosen it. During Lillian's first year of living with the McGuires, Marnie had taken to teasing her about working all the time and never dating. Dr. McGuire had overheard one of those discussions and made a remark that Lillian was just a free single lady and Marnie should leave her alone. Then Lillian had stood up and given a horrible rendition of "Single Ladies" that reduced everyone to tears of laughter. Dr. McGuire assumed she had just made it up because he'd never heard the song. She pulled it up on her iTunes, and he was surprised to hear it was a real song by a real artist. He looked at her phone and recognized the picture. He was familiar with Beyoncé's image but not her music. "Oh, *her*," he had said. A sharp look from Marnie elicited the hasty correction from Al, "I'm sorry, who is that?"

"Oh shut up," Marnie jokingly snapped.

The professor barely mumbled under his breath, "I'm old but I ain't dead."

"What did you say?"

"I think I'm getting a little cold in my head"

Lillian loved watching the two of them go back in forth. From that day on, "Single Ladies" was Doc's ringtone.

———

She answered the phone with a question. "Dr. McGuire?"

A surprisingly jovial voice responded, "Yes, it sure is. How have you been, Lil Man?"

Lillian had not heard that nickname in months and the sound of it made her smile. "I'm fine. I've just been worried silly about you. Are you okay? I've rarely seen your car at the house, and someone said you were spending ungodly hours at your lab."

"Yes, that's true. But it's been for a good reason. Ever since Marnie … was taken from me, I've had an empty spot of course. I had no idea how I would fill it. One day I knew what I had to do. Lil Man, I just have to put all of my efforts into finding a way to neutralize this virus on a large scale," he lied. "I can work uninhibited by grant limitations and institutional competition. It can just be my contribution dedicated to Marnie's memory. I just may need a little bit of help from you."

"From me?"

"Yes. Look, let me take you to dinner and we can talk."

"I'm on call this Friday. I will be off Saturday evening. Why don't we make it special? Let me treat you to dinner at that place on Birch this Saturday night."

The conversation was a strange one. The two were talking like they were in two different cities, but they lived in the same house. Yet it was true that they would likely not see each other until the evening of their planned dinner.

"How about eight o'clock?" Dr. McGuire inquired.

"That sounds fine." Lillian clicked off.

Maybe he would be all right after all. Maybe this newfound purpose would be instrumental in restoring his brilliant mind. Maybe he would actually find a way to diminish the effects of the virus. Maybe he would leave a lasting legacy in Marnie's name. She smiled and laid back on the bed, comforted by her thoughts. Her "dad" was going to be okay after all.

29

AL HATED LYING TO LIL MAN. BUT THERE WAS NO WAY AROUND it. If he came right out and asked for what he wanted, no, *needed*, from her, then not only would she refuse to do it but she would also lecture him about the ethics of revenge. It was also necessary to keep her in the dark for her own protection. The less she knew, the less someone could assign any amount of blame or responsibility to her. Her life and career were just starting. His were over, except for one notable task yet to be accomplished. He could not in good conscience jeopardize Lil.

The restaurant wasn't crowded. Guidelines were set up such that seating had to be dramatically reduced to account for the social distancing measures. There were no large parties, and distance was maintained between tables. Like many notable stop-offs for celebrities, the restaurant featured walls lined with the photographs of famous people who visited and left autographed pictures. There were athletes, movie personalities, and even one former president. Al mused that the whole restaurant must have been shut down that night and only Secret Service members could eat. He remembered a celebratory dinner he had attended some years before. Marnie had not been with him that night, so he sat in one of the single seats at a table of ten. He struck up a conversation with the nice young man seated next to him. The young man turned out to be Secret Service. Intrigued, Al asked if there were more agents present, to which the young man answered in the affirmative. When Al asked "Where?" the agent just smiled and looked away.

Al's replay of the memory stopped abruptly as the host inquired about his reservation and asked if he would like to be seated or to wait for his guest. Al said he would like to wait so they could be seated together. A few minutes later Lillian came through the door.

"Lil Man!"

Lillian looked toward Al's direction and what she saw startled her. But she skillfully hid her shock and responded, "Dr. McGuire! It's been too long."

Looking at him more closely now, her heart sank. She gave the elderly man a long hug, the hug of a daughter who hurts for her infirm father. Dr. McGuire had never been a sharp dresser, but his appearance had at least always been neat. Now he was standing in an upscale restaurant wearing a wrinkled shirt and dusty shoes. Lillian also detected the faint odor of cooking. She knew he had not been preparing meals, so it only meant that his clothes had not been laundered in quite some time.

"Let's have a seat," Lillian said gently. They looked at the host, proceeded to their table, and sat down.

"She always got the salmon," the professor stated flatly. Though he was looking at the menu, he wasn't really seeing it.

"I know," Lillian replied. "I remember." She saw heartache and grief every day, but this was different. This was Al. Marnie's Al.

Halfway through the meal, Al began to drop half-truths into the conversation, establishing the foundation for his delicate request. "I'm back in my lab more than ever now. Many nights I just sleep there and come home in the morning and change clothes. I just don't want to be at the house very much anymore." His eyes welled up. Then the half-truths morphed into outright falsehoods. "I am going to find a whole new approach to fighting this plague. I am going to dedicate my discoveries to Marnie's memory. I am going to genetically alter the virus' RNA. I will develop a competing strain that functions very much like cowpox worked to mitigate smallpox. The process is a bit out of the box, so I am not expecting much help from the university."

Of course Lillian understood his reference to smallpox. In her first-year medical history class, she had learned about Edward Jenner, a physician who discovered in 1796 that smallpox seemed to have little penetration into the population of milkmaids. Because these milking ladies frequently contracted cowpox. a virus similar to smallpox, the women developed an immunity to both pathogens. When the sores from cowpox lesions were scraped and the contents injected into another person, that person gained a degree of immunity from smallpox. Jenner's discovery was widely accepted as the origin of the smallpox vaccine, but Lillian later learned that the art of vaccination had been practiced in Africa nearly one hundred years before Jenner. Sitting there in the restaurant listening to Dr. McGuire, Lillian understood immediately that he was proposing a similar strategy against Q47cx. If a milder competing virus could take its place, perhaps the mortality rate would not be as high.

Lillian wondered about the validity of Dr. McGuire's experimental design, but she knew her medical and clinical training was far less theoretical than that of an accomplished molecular biologist. She thought it through as best she could and concluded that it might just be possible. Even if it took years, at least it would give a man laid low by grief something to do. She reached across the table and touched his hand.

"That's wonderful, Doc. How can I help? You said you needed something from me."

"I need a sample of the actual wild strain of the virus. I could probably petition it through the department but that would require months of paperwork and red tape. There would be tracking and numbers and it would just take too long. We need action right now. I just need one small sample."

Feeling uncomfortable, Lillian countered, "That sounds interesting Doc, but what do you hope to accomplish?"

"I am going to alter the genomic sequence using CAGET technology. Are you familiar with it?"

Lillian could vaguely remember having heard the word, but at that point in her life, the basic sciences were three years and ten thousand patients behind her.

"It rings a bell, but I'm not sure how it works."

"The method allows for specific fragments of genetic material to be substituted for others. So one could make a mutation that is much less deadly. Then again, if one were so inclined, I guess you could make a mutation that was much *more* deadly," the professor murmured.

Lillian stopped eating for a split second and glanced at the professor. He had a slightly strange look on his face. Had he betrayed a thought he had not meant to say?

"But of course no one would consider anything like that," he hastily added.

Changing the subject, he began to reminisce about times past. Searching Lillian's face, Al asked her, "Have you ever been parasailing?"

"No."

"Well I have. But only once. It was one of those times when you start lying to God."

"Lying to God?"

"Sure. You are way up there in the air, behind this boat. Just sailing hundreds of feet above the ground. You then start lying. You say, 'God, if you ever let me get down from here I will never do anything out of your will again.' You know you are lying but you just want to get down!"

The two laughed. The professor had not laughed in weeks.

"She got me up there!" Al continued. "We were walking on the beach on one of our very few vacations, and there was a little shack where they offered parasailing. I didn't notice, but Marnie did. She said, 'Oh that looks like fun! Let's do it.' I laughed thinking she was joking, but she wasn't." The professor lost just a bit of his joviality as he continued. "She was the adventurous one. But I couldn't let her know that I was scared to death to get on that thing. So I played brave and got on. We did a tandem sail. It was good that she was in the front because she could not see the pure terror in my eyes." The professor's eyes slightly glazed over. "She was my life, Lil. They took my life away. Somebody needs to pay."

Lillian could not quite explain her feelings. On the one hand she felt such sympathy for Doc. She could feel the pain surging through his words, and she felt it bone deep. On the other hand, a tiny morsel of unease crept into her consciousness. "Somebody needs to pay," he'd said. The thought of retribution for a loved one's illness was foreign to Lillian. She dismissed it as a distracted utterance from a grieving husband, but his words still left her uneasy.

They finished the meal rather quietly, and Lillian promised Al that she would see what she could do. She was not at all comfortable with the request, but Doc's reasons seemed noble. Almost against her will, Lillian's quick imagination conceived a plan of how to retrieve the sample without losing her license. When she realized that it was possible, she gasped. What was she doing, thinking of committing a crime? But this was Dr. McGuire. Her brilliant surrogate father who wanted to save thousands of lives in the name of the woman she would forever think of as her mother. She had to do it. Maybe Doc's sanity even hinged on keeping busy. It had to be done. She opened the door to her Supra and climbed inside.

30

ON THE WAY TO THE HOSPITAL, LILLIAN THOUGHT ABOUT HOW the chaos caused by the virus would work in her favor. These days, the intensive care unit beds were never empty. As soon as a room was vacated due to discharge or death, within the hour it was filled. At times the retrievers from the morgue would make combination runs. In an effort to try and hold on to some degree of sanity, the staff constantly cracked jokes to each other. When Lillian needed to laugh, her co-worker Tasha, a slightly older ICU nurse, was her favorite sparring partner. Tasha was a consummate professional, but she also had the best punchlines on the ward. Lillian decided to smuggle the virus out of the hospital on a day when Tasha was working. She would need the comic relief both to deflect suspicion and calm her own nerves. For the moment though, she could just enjoy her friend's company.

"You know, Tash, I'm starting to really worry. I'm not sure how much longer we can keep this up."

"I know. My husband's mother is a diabetic with asthma. Every day we're just praying she stays healthy."

"I don't know how you do it, dealing with this madness while sustaining a marriage and a child. I'm so tired when I get home, I don't have anything left to take care of my baby."

"Your *baby?*"

"Sure. She spends so much time alone now that I'm afraid she'll forget me."

Tasha froze, racking her brain, trying to figure out when Dr. Manning could have had a child.

"But at least she remembers all the things I taught her," Lillian continued, deadpan. "She can still do zero to sixty in 4.1 seconds."

"Oh girl." The nurse pushed her shoulder and let out a short, sharp burst of laughter. Formal titles had long ago been dispatched as they were all just combatants in the same war now.

Getting a wild strain of the virus out of the hospital would not be easy for Lillian, as she had to violate safeguards to accomplish the task. Each morning the staff were assigned personal protective equipment, or PPE, for the day. The PPE consisted of a jumpsuit-like covering, a face shield, and an N95 mask. Multiple pairs of non-latex examination gloves were available in each room and outside the unit. The trick would be to get a sample of the virus out of the ICU while not contaminating any area outside the restricted one. Items that had to be used in the ICU but later taken out were pushed through a small, recently installed revolving hatch so they could be retrieved on the other side after sanitation.

When leaving the unit for the day, one or more staff members would enter a room and remove all of the protective equipment, stripping down to a plain scrub suit. The equipment had to be taken off carefully so that it remained inside out. That way, all of the exposed surfaces remained facing the inside, hidden from exposure. The items then went through the hatch and were sanitized before being rotated—now uncontaminated—back to the staff members. The recently stripped professionals could then retrieve their items. So Lillian had to get a contained sample of the virus out of the ICU without sending it through the hatch, while making absolutely sure the sample did not contaminate anything. Otherwise she would contribute to further spread of the virus. Tubes for viral cultures were readily available in a lab area down the hall.

The morning of the attempt, Lillian arrived at the unit a bit early. While still dressed in street clothes, she walked to the lab and picked up a couple of culture tubes. She placed one in each pocket of her scrubs. She dressed herself in PPE and entered the unit. The plan she had seen in a flash at the restaurant was now underway. Sitting at the table across from Doc, she had realized that volunteering to suction a patient would be the easiest way to get what he needed. Suctioning patients produced the largest exposure to infected mucous and secretions, and although respiratory therapists usually suctioned the ventilator-dependent patients, it was not at all unusual for everyone to pitch in.

Halfway through her shift, Lillian agreed to help one of the respiratory therapists. The suctioning produced the usual spray of infected fluid, and instead of wiping the mucous off her face shield immediately, Lillian took a cotton swab and saturated the tip in it. Palming the swab in her gloved hand, she made it known she needed a second glove.

"Damn," she lied. "Got a hole in my glove."

She was given another glove and carefully placed it over the first, holding the new one only by the outside, so that she never touched its inner lining. That way, she ensured the sample of viral particles would not be contaminated by any other microbes. Now she had a small swab inside a clean glove. Lillian then maneuvered the position of the small swab to align with a finger so she could continue to work. In a way, her sleight-of-hand was similar to what magicians do every day. She exited the unit at the end of the shift, peeling off her contaminated clothing in the decontamination room while holding onto the glove and swab. Once she was out of her space suit, she reached into her pocket and took out a small vial of transport medium. She opened the top of the bottle and pushed the swab through the glove and into the vial. The punctured glove was left behind with the other contaminated items to be disposed of by the designated crew. She pocketed the vial and left. The second vial was just a backup. She would dispose of it harmlessly in the trash.

31

THOUGH QUITE AN ACCOMPLISHMENT, THE ACQUISITION OF wild virus in a culture tube was just the beginning. Al knew there was much more to be done. The next three to four weeks would be a non-stop marathon of planning and timely execution, but the professor was no stranger to long hours. During his graduate school years he had burned the midnight oil countless times. Al's mind drifted back to one of those long nights in his first year of graduate school. It had been a critical night that impacted his life in ways he never could have foreseen.

Alton McGuire entered graduate school as an idealistic prospective scientist, confident he would rank near the top of his class. With such a high ranking, he had imagined, he would go on to be offered international postdoctoral fellowships that would take him all over the world. But he was not arrogant or entitled. He expected his education to demand blood, sweat, and tears, and he had never minded hard work. He also knew that two heads are better than one, so, like many of his fellow graduate students, he joined forces with a couple of study buddies. Al's group included three other students: Olivia, an extremely bright and attractive young woman from a small school in Kentucky, Chris, a former pharmacist from a tough area of Chicago, and Gary, a

Japanese American student who wanted to return to his community and start a bioethics department at the local college.

Olivia had been a former beauty queen at her university and possessed a brain to match her outward appearance. More than once she had been underestimated by male counterparts, who subsequently found themselves academically cut down like stalks of sugar cane. Chris, the pharmacist, was quite a bit older. He had worked in a tough area of Chicago and also had the distinction of adding undercover narcotics agent to his resume. Stories of his exploits as an ex-cop always kept Al fascinated. But Gary's stories were chilling. He recounted to the group how his own grandparents had been interred in the Japanese camps during World War II. His grandfather had owned a small business and his grandmother was a schoolteacher. The bitter stories of their removal and relocation had left Gary with a sardonic sensibility that resonated with Al and his memories of the segregated South.

One night, the four of them were huddled in their usual study cove on the eve of a huge biochemistry examination, one of the two to be given that semester. They met regularly in a small storage closet at the end of a long hallway. The closet was on the same floor where classes were held but after hours no one ever came toward that direction. They usually took a five-minute break every hour until about one in the morning and then headed home. This particular night everyone headed out at the usual time, but Al decided he would stay a while longer to nail down a few more concepts. Olivia warned him that the test would start at ten the next morning and she better not come in and find him asleep in that closet. He looked at her and promised. Al was the youngest in the group and Olivia looked out for him. She was only two years older, but still treated him like a younger brother. Al appreciated that.

About one thirty Al felt his concentration drifting. He decided to go for his usual stay-awake special. A vending machine down the opposite end of an L-shaped hallway contained his favorite remedy: a twelve-ounce Dr. Pepper. Al stood up and stretched. He was happy he had put the change from his last trip to the machine in his pocket so the thirty cents for his elixir would not be a challenge to find. Taking a slow walk down the long hallway, stretching as he walked, Al thought he heard voices. He stopped and rounded the corner cautiously. He peered down the hallway past the vending machine alcove and saw that there was a light coming from the very last classroom on that end of the hall. Al walked quietly down the hallway on his toes, careful not to make heel-clicking noises on the tile floor. The door was closed but each door was equipped with a vertical six-inch window with smoked glass. The window was apparently purposed to let late arriving students peer in to know when to enter.

Al peered in, unnoticed, from the hallway. Seated inside was a group of students who Al recognized. He didn't know them by name, but they were all members of the same biochemistry class as he was, the class with the test tomorrow. They were all paying close attention to the instruction, but Al could not see who was talking. Eventually the instructor stepped into view allowing Al to see his face. To Al's shock, it was Professor Gerald Fitzpatrick, the professor who would be administering the test less than eight hours later. With incredulity Al listened for a short while but could only hear bits and pieces of the instruction. One overheard sentence shocked him. "Now if the question asks …" he heard Dr. Fitzpatrick say.

Al slowly and quietly backed away from the window. Tomorrow's test would be graded on a curve. How could he finish near the top of the class if the instructor was giving private lessons to a select group of his classmates just a few hours before the test? Al thought of going in and saying, "Hi guys, sorry I'm late." But he realized such a bold move would backfire. No matter how good his grades were during the first two years of coursework, his final years of graduate school would require a lot of very subjective evaluation by Dr. Fitzpatrick, his major professor. He could not and would not jeopardize his future by calling attention to himself as a troublemaker. He tiptoed away from the door, forgetting his Dr. Pepper. Then he gathered his things and went home.

32

PROFESSOR FITZPATRICK WOULD NEVER KNOW IT, BUT HE would go on to play a crucial role in Al's plan to avenge Marnie. In 1983 a group of researchers, including one of the professor's graduate students, began to try to make animal models more closely resemble human tissues. Looking at various immunodeficiency disorders, the researchers realized they needed to test potential medications and therapies by using animals that would mimic human responses. When Al had read the first journal articles about "humanized mice," he'd recognized the name at the top and shuddered, remembering Professor Fitzpatrick's betrayal. But he was impressed that the team had used mice with blank immune systems and injected them with human stem cells to produce tissues that would perform like human tissues.

"Hello?" the young woman with the FedEx uniform interrupted Al's thoughts. "I need to have someone sign for this."

Dr. McGuire signed his name on the electronic device.

"No," the woman said, "I need you to sign *your* name if you are accepting it. You can't sign Dr. McGuire's name."

Al felt the bile bubble in his belly as he reached inside his shirt pocket and flipped out his university ID. Less than a second later, he saw the familiar trio of shock, embarrassment, and remorse ripple across her face.

"Oh, I'm sorry I was just ... I didn't know ... I thought ..."

Al smiled and bid her good day. "The more things change, the more they stay the same," he muttered to himself.

The oversized crate was labeled CAUTION: LIVE ANIMALS. Al's plans were taking shape, and the humanized mice were the last component. He surveyed the items that had already arrived: numerous small cages, mouse rations, water dispensers, and a carton of twenty-four tiny, red motion sensor lights purchased from an electronics store. He had also ordered online a small 3D printer that had been sent to his house instead of the lab. For the next five days, Al functioned more like a carpenter than a research scientist, but the hard labor was necessary. The plan required him to construct three long platforms so that the cages could be spaced one foot apart on each platform. Then he outfitted each cage with a feeding tray, a water dispenser, and a small motion sensor light. He placed soft mats on the bottom of each cage.

In addition to building the mouse accommodations, Al had installed a closed-circuit camera purchased from an alarm company. The camera kept the cages in focus at all times. With an app on his phone he could see the cages from anywhere in the city. Because mice are nocturnal animals, Al could not observe them closely enough without staying in the lab overnight and arousing suspicion. So, over the next three weeks, while the mice lived a luxurious life with all the food they could eat and fresh water every day, Al worked like a dog and slept very little.

Back at the house, Al carefully assembled the 3D printer. Muttering benign curses under his breath, he asked himself how in the world the same geniuses who had invented the technology couldn't figure out how to send it in one piece to their customers. He squinted at the user manual and struggled with the tiny screws and components until he finally heard the hum of the functioning machine. One day after the arrival of the printer, a small box containing a lock pick set was delivered. Al was astounded that a tool specifically designed for criminal activity could be purchased so easily online. But instead of allowing himself to ruminate over internet commerce regulation, he got back to work and scrolled through internet search engine results, trying to figure out which material to order for the printer. After reading that polycarbonate is the strongest substance that can be molded by a 3D printer, Al ordered a small batch of filaments.

33

THE NEVER-ENDING TIDE OF CRITICALLY ILL PATIENTS HAD finally started to recede. Lillian had more days away from the hospital, and she took advantage of her time off by spending much of it at home. She continued to regularly check whether the professor was there, but he rarely was. So, still sticking to her decontamination ritual, she allowed herself more freedom in her use of the house. She had even taken to curling up on the big comfy sofa where Marnie used to sit watching television. But she was careful never to sit there if she was sleepy. She could not risk Dr. McGuire arriving home and finding her asleep in Marnie's spot. Lillian knew that Doc loved her like a daughter, but he loved Marnie more. His grief was so raw and all-consuming during that period that Lillian knew if he perceived any disrespect to his wife's memory, consequences for the offender would be swift and terrible. But she craved a feeling of closeness to Marnie, and her risk of getting caught was low because it appeared that Doc was rarely at home. In actuality Lillian was in little danger of being discovered. Al was at his lab night and day.

He had put a rush on the delivery of the mice. At first, he had not been able acquire humanized mice because they were special order. When Lillian had handed the virus to him weeks ago, suspended in transport media, both of them knew it had to be placed in live host within seven days. So Al had decided to just use half a dozen stock mice to do the job, with no intention of using them in the final experiments. He would dispose of them now that the humanized mice had arrived.

Al's plan also required a milder species of virus that he would use to manipulate the lethality of Q47cx however he wanted to. Viruses that were considered harmless could be obtained from the stock supplies in the department. Those samples were kept growing and safe in tissue culture containers. That way, they were available for research on demand. No one had a problem with Dr. McGuire checking out samples of a few types of herpes viruses. After all, how much trouble could they cause? The research stock room assistant had no idea of the potential threat he had released to Professor Alton McGuire.

The university's prize genetic sequencing unit was a four hundred thousand dollar masterpiece kept under lock and key. The unit was able to determine the genetic code of many viruses simultaneously in a relatively rapid fashion. Besides determining the genetic codes, the unit could insert, delete, and rearrange base pairs to create new genetic material. Al took the calculated step of becoming friendly with the chief researcher in order to better understand the apparatus.

Dr. Clifton Bales was proud of his toy. He was the only one within three hundred miles who had the means to swiftly sequence genes and carry out CAGET (Comprehensive Advanced Gene Editing Tool) gene editing. He never missed an opportunity to expound upon the unit's capabilities to anyone who would listen. Most people wanted to hear the Cliff notes version because Dr. Bales was not the most animated speaker. So when he found someone who really wanted to hear his spiel, he could drone on for hours. Al easily slipped into the role of the eager student and soaked up all of the finer points of capability and procedure from Dr. Bales.

On those rare occasions when Dr. Bales asked *him* a question, Al explained that he was working on a project to mitigate the effects and virulence of particular viruses by stimulating the body's own natural immunity. He did not want to develop a vaccine but rather enhance the body's own responsiveness. Sharing research data showing lower death rates in women after viral infection than in men, Al soon had Dr. Bales on board with his theory that enhancing the adrenal glands' response at the time of infection could save lives. Because the adrenal gland is the site of estradiol synthesis, which leads directly to the production of estrogen, this enhanced estrogen effect could blunt the lethal capability of some viruses. Al explained that there was at least one virus that tended to attack the adrenal gland more than others did, stimulating an especially vigorous response. That virus was the herpes virus. Intrigued by Al's theories, Dr. Bales thought it was an interesting project.

"Well I'm really busy with my own work but would be happy to help with some of the resequencing if you need me," Dr. Bales offered.

"That would be fantastic," Al said with relief.

Though Al was at peace with his ultimate goal, the act of deliberate deception was still something he struggled with. He had struggled with lying to Lil Man and he was struggling now. He had never quite been on board with Machiavelli's doctrine. Did the ends really justify the means? Somehow, using bits of truth to make his lies more believable felt more egregious to him than a more extravagant deceit might have. Truth interwoven with lies, making those lies more powerful and dangerous … Al marveled how similar it was to a mild virus carrying the poison of a deadly one. Or his love for Marnie inspiring an act of mass destruction. He squeezed his eyes tightly shut to put a stop to his thoughts. The monster had to be destroyed.

A picture of a small sailboat hung on the wall behind Dr. Bales's desk. One afternoon as he and Al were heading back to their respective offices, Al asked him, "Is that your boat?"

"Oh heavens no," Dr. Bales replied. "It belongs to my brother. He purchased it about three years ago for his son. His son was diagnosed with multiple sclerosis, so being on the water is the only time he feels free. My brother says there's just something about the motion of the waves he finds soothing. My brother is a manager at a hardware store and just barely gets by, but he wanted to get that boat for his boy. He worked long nights as a security guard for months to get it. And he says it's worth every penny."

A kid with multiple sclerosis, Al thought. If he got this virus, he would be dead in days. The guilt crashed onto Al like an avalanche. He was plotting a scheme that could well result in this innocent child's death. He knew he at least had to stress to Bales to take every precaution to keep the boy safe. "Does your brother know that his son must stay inside and away from people all the time?" Al asked.

Dr. Bales, slightly puzzled, assumed Al was worried about his nephew's time out on the water. "They only take the boat out on weekends and it's just the two of them."

"Well, make sure to remind both of them to frequently wash their hands well and wear masks," Al admonished.

He fought his conflicting emotions and stared at the photo for a long while. He imagined a little blond kid sitting in an adaptive wheelchair with an LSU baseball cap perched on his head. He pictured the boy's delight in his weekly excursion on the water with his father. For a minute Al considered scrapping the whole project and returning home. Then, like an early morning fog, a mist clouded over his inner vision, and the image of a cottonmouth faded into view.

"Al! Al!" His companion interrupted the trance. "Where were you? You were staring at that picture and looked to be a thousand miles away."

"Sorry," Al said. "Let's swap some base pairs."

34

AL EXPLAINED TO DR. BALES THAT IF HE COULD JUST REMOVE the right base pairs from the herpes virus—which tended to attack the adrenals—and insert them into Q47cx, then the modified version of Q47cx would stimulate the adrenal glands. As a result, the enhanced immune response from the adrenals would weaken the *unmodified* virus's effect, thus bringing a swift end to the pandemic. Dr. Bales was skeptical of Al's hypothesis and thought the plan was a longshot, but he also knew that nothing else had been able to stop Q47cx, and so any approach was worth a try. Al went to retrieve his samples of the herpes virus and Q47cx. Dr. Bales raised an eyebrow. How on earth had this guy gotten his hands on Q47cx, he wondered. Though suspicious of Al's explanation of how he had acquired the wild strain of the virus, Dr. Bales knew that sometimes who you know is better than what you know. He assumed Al had likely paid off a lab tech.

Each time a new spliced virus was produced—a new version of Q47cx carrying a bit of genetic information from the herpes virus—Al would inoculate two of the humanized mice with the new viral sample. Records would be kept of how long it took for them to become ill, or to succumb to the novel virus. The mice that survived long after the viral inoculation, or even recovered, were carrying the viral variants that showed the greater promise. At least that is what Al allowed Dr. Bales to believe. It was almost the truth, as the most convincing lies are. Al and Bales began spending an hour or so a day on the project. As the weeks passed, Dr. Bales's interest continued to increase as he considered the possibilities of a successful experiment. He knew that Al had no interest in publishing, so if there was a major breakthrough, he would receive most of the credit.

Al designed a rather novel, if crude, way of determining the how quickly the mice died, as well as their precise time of death. Each cage was equipped with a motion sensor. Each motion sensor was attached to a tiny red light. Mice are nocturnal animals. They rarely move around in the daytime but are very active at night. During the day Al kept the area where the mice were kept in bright light. He focused a closed-circuit camera on the entire span of cages. The camera was equipped with a time stamp. Al inoculated each mouse with a different sample of spliced Q47cx virus. When Al would leave the lab in the late evening, often just to take a nap in the lounge area, the cameras were turned on. All of the cages showed activity as each red indicator light was detectable from the closed-circuit camera. The following morning, he would turn the lights back on, mimicking daylight, and check the conditions of the humanized mice. He would make observations as to which were sick, and which showed signs of recovery.

For the first three nights, all of the red indicator lights remained on, indicating that all of the mice were quite active. By night number four, the time-lapse mode of the closed-circuit camera showed there were periods when the lights turned off before later coming back on. Taking note of the cages where this phenomenon occurred, Al would examine those mice first the next day. Without fail he discovered that the flickering lights indicated there had been considerably decreased movement. The mice were becoming ill. When the lights did not come on at all, or went out and stayed out, the next morning Al would discover the mice had died. The correlation to the indicator lights was one hundred percent. Dissecting the mice, Al discovered that the adrenal glands of the dead mice were nearly destroyed. The substituted base pairs in those RNA strands were lethal. Now he only needed to determine how lethal by looking at the times of death.

Just to be certain, Al did a second run of the same experiment to corroborate his findings. Sure enough, he replicated his results. Rapid lethality with certain of the combinations and almost complete recovery with others. Al only had one small problem. He had shown his data to be reproducible under the ever curious and watchful eye of his self-appointed associate. Bales would race to the research board with the findings, and there would be a year-long investigation. It was possible that there really could be a decrease in the lethality of the viral infection, and millions could be spared. The lies he had told Dr. Torres and Lil could become the truth. He could wrest control of his work back from Bales and Steichen, dedicate the research to Marnie's memory, and—a sharp pain seized Al's head and neck as he suddenly had a vision of Marnie with a cottonmouth coiled around her entire body. The pain subsided, the vision faded, and Al returned to his work.

The mice in most of the cages lasted at least ten to twelve days; half of those showed complete recovery. The mice in three of the cages lasted only seven days before dying. But the mice in cage 4 lasted only forty-eight hours each time. To prove the rapid lethality of mixture number four, Al did the experiment one final time using only two mice and inoculating them with viral variant 4. He did not depend on the red indicator lights this time. After twenty-four hours he stayed to watch. The mice began to cough and make a very faint squeaking sound. It was the equivalent of a congested wheeze in a human subject. The mice, within hours of each other, convulsed and foamed at the mouth. Death followed. Death of the first in twenty-one hours. Death of the second in twenty-three. Al had found the most lethal of all of the combinations. It was time to go to work.

At six o'clock the next morning, long before Dr. Bales would arrive, Al was already in the lab. In reality the mice in cage 4 had died of a rapidly lethal virus, while the mice in cage 15 were completely healthy and totally recovered. So Al changed the cage numbers, placing cage-4 markers on cage 15 and cage-15 markers on cage 4. He then did the same with the inoculum tubes containing the viral variants. The official story for Bales was that if humans responded as the humanized mice had, then the inoculation in cage 15 could be the breakthrough they had been hoping for. Upon Bales's arrival, he eagerly announced his results. Al explained that the next step was harvesting viral strain 15 for possible use as a vaccine. But in actuality, Al would be harvesting strain 4, the deadliest strain of all. The savvy professor was careful to refer to "our work" and "our breakthrough," appealing to Bales's ego. It worked. Bales was so busy thinking of all the publications and prizes in his future that he congratulated Al and never suspected a thing.

Al continued the charade. "We should sit tight for a few weeks though. I'd like to do some more confirmations to strengthen our case before we say a word to anyone. We wouldn't want to be caught with egg on our face, not for something this important." Bringing his performance for Bales to a fever pitch, he consciously brought counterfeit tears to his eyes. "I'm doing this for Marnie you know."

He had finally spoken some truth.

35

ALTHOUGH SURGES OF THE VIRUS CONTINUED TO RIPPLE through the population, the pressure to open the economy was too great. There were staged reopenings, allowing for a decreased capacity in public places and outside seating in some restaurants. Despite the government's guidelines, and the expert advice of noted virologists and epidemiologists, crowds formed everywhere. Attitudes toward the social distancing guidelines divided communities, friends, and even family. Al marveled at how rapidly science had become a political football, as the idea of absolute truth had become debatable. At every turn, in every corner of public life, he saw the slow deterioration of every measure that could halt the spread of the virus. These fools deserved their fate.

Allowed to open at half-capacity, the Louisiana Sports Arena had quickly returned to prominence as a beacon for young men. The arena had begun to book events, only selling every other seat. It was a non-sensical policy because when a family purchased tickets, once inside the arena they simply moved to whichever seats they preferred. There were not enough ushers to enforce the guidelines, so the whole matter of social distancing was moot. One of the first events was a children's ice show. Sure that the tickets would sell out quickly because quarantined children had been cooped up for so long, Al was one of the first in the walk-up ticket line. He was aware that tickets could be purchased online, but he made an in-person, cash-only ticket purchase for a reason.

Unknown to most people, a picture is taken of them approximately fifty times a day. Adding up the images taken by security cameras, traffic cameras, and mapping cameras, fifty times a day might even be an underestimation. Having read an article about it some years previous, Al was taking no chances. He donned a wide brimmed hat and a pair of cheap sunglasses purchased from a drug store. Once at the ticket window, he requested two sets of tickets. Making small talk with the ticket operator through the secure glass, he joked about bringing his grandson one night and his wife bringing the granddaughter the next. He purchased tickets for the Thursday night and Saturday night performances. Having paid cash for the tickets, he headed home.

With his 3D printer, Al fashioned and printed a very small but very sharp tool. The tool was a wire cutter. He knew the alloy used to make the instrument would not show up on the metal detector scan performed at the arena and that fact was essential. On Tuesday, he went to his bank and drew out one thousand dollars in cash. He asked for the cash in the form of twenty fifty-dollar bills. On Wednesday, he returned to his bank and again drew out twenty fifty-dollar bills, this time careful to use a different teller and withdraw from a different account.

Al arrived at the arena a little early on Thursday night but waited in his vehicle. He was able to park in the attached garage and comfortably waited for the bulk of the audience, mostly parents with screaming children, to arrive. In his pockets were the two stacks of fifty-dollar bills and the small wire cutter. Approximately twenty minutes before show time, the arena became more crowded and noisier. Al departed his vehicle and made his way toward the arena's entrance. Upon arrival, he was given a small blue bowl in which to place all of his items that could potentially set off the metal detector. Al placed his watch and cell phone along with his wallet in the bowl and handed it to the attendant. He stepped through the archway and to his shock the arch buzzed and flashed a red light.

"Step back through," the attendant commanded.

Al stepped back and tried again. Again, the buzzer sounded, and light flashed.

"Do you have any metal in your pockets, sir?" the monotonous voice inquired.

Al frantically patted his pockets. His keys were gone. Then it dawned on him what the problem could be. "It must be the belt," he reassured the attendant. He pulled the belt with the large buckle off his trousers and placed it on the table. He stepped through a third time and again the buzzer sounded.

"Sir, you will need to step over here and we will have to wand you."

He reluctantly stepped to the side and another security officer appeared with a hand wand. Small beads of sweat were starting to form on Al's forehead. He would have no trouble explaining the wire-cutting tool, but it would surely be confiscated. He needed it for the rest of his plan. He stepped to the side and reached inside his pocket. The paddle wand was waved over his arms and shoulders. When it reached his pocket, it beeped.

"Something in that pocket sir?" the guard asked.

Al reached inside his pocket wondering how he could hide his device. Then his hand brushed against something hard and flat. It was the key to Dr. Bales's lab. He had never placed it on his ring but had just kept it loose in his pocket. As the security agent raised the wand, Al said, "Oops! I got it." He produced the key from his pocket and laid it on the table. The wand passed over the pocket again. Quiet. He was in.

36

AL CHECKED TO MAKE SURE THE TWO STACKS OF FIFTY-DOLLAR
bills were still in place. He walked around the circular concourse toward
the section where his seat was. The smell of popcorn was thick in the
air, mingled with the slightly oily smell of french fries. The high-pitched
squeals from the inside most likely corresponded with some well-prac-
ticed acrobatic leap. The sounds were almost musical. No wonder
Marnie loved kids the way she did. Al was once again thankful that
studies had shown little to no serious effects on children from the virus.
He wondered if it was God's way of punishing the ones actually responsible for the world's decline, but that was a philosophical argument for
another day.

He wandered the arena corridors until the show had been in progress
for approximately twenty minutes. The timing was important. Having
just started, the show would keep the attention of the little ones for at
least half an hour. More importantly, the ten-dollar sodas their parents
had purchased would not have made their way through the children's
systems and into their bladders yet. The bathrooms would be empty. Al
turned into one the bathrooms just off the circular concourse. As he had
predicted, there was no one there. Then his ear caught a subtle rustling

sound, and his gaze turned toward it. He had been mistaken. There was one pair in the restroom just finishing up at the sink. A little girl with a ponytail and an older gentleman, most likely her grandfather. Modern arenas were equipped with family restrooms, but the aging Louisiana Sports Arena had no such amenities. Al stayed out of sight until they headed toward the door.

Once the restroom was empty Al quickly ducked into a stall. Locking the door behind him, he removed the alloy wire cutter from his pocket and placed it on the toilet tissue dispenser. Climbing onto the toilet seat he was just tall enough to reach the light fixture. The older arena had a standard florescent light fixture with elongated bulbs. Each end snapped into place with two prongs. Al snapped the cover off and pulled and twisted the bulb. He left one in while he grabbed the wire cutter. If he pulled on the now vacant fixture end where the bulb had been, he could see a tiny exposed portion of the wire leading to the fixture. He guided the alloy wire cutter into the small slot and clipped the wire. The fixture went dark immediately. Under most circumstances the electrical current would have produced a shock, but Al was standing on a porcelain non-conducting fixture and had clipped the wire with a non-conducting alloy.

He stepped down from the toilet and straightened his clothes. Walking back into the concourse he spied an usher. He informed the usher that one of the lights in the restroom wasn't working and that someone could have an accident if they weren't careful. The usher dutifully informed him that she would call maintenance. Al moved out of sight and proceeded to one of the vending stands. He ordered and paid for a soda but remained near the restroom entrance. Ten minutes later a middle-aged man appeared. He was balding and clean-shaven. He carried with him a toolbox and a long florescent light bulb. Within fifteen minutes he emerged from the restroom. Al quickly peered inside. The light was back on.

When Al saw that the light was repaired, he knew this was not the night to carry out his plan. It was a weeknight. He should have known. Throughout the five-day week, the A team would be in place. Experienced workers, most likely full-time. Clearly the maintenance man he had just observed was a professional, able to repair the small clipped wire quickly with no problem. As the repairman had exited the bathroom, he had even carried a backup unused bulb with him. Al knew he would have to make another trip to the arena. He would end up using his Saturday ticket after all. He left the arena and headed home.

Two nights later he returned. Arriving about the same time as he had on Thursday night, he chose to park on the opposite end of the arena. Again he carried with him the bills and the wire cutter, but this time he entered the gate from the opposite end of the concourse. He had drawn a little attention to himself on Thursday and did not want to arouse any suspicion. It was unlikely, but Al wasn't interested in taking any chances. This time he was meticulous in making sure there was no metal in his pockets and breezed past security with no problems. His ticket was taken, and he made his way once again to the concourse. At approximately the same time during the show, he went into the restroom. It was all clear. He entered and locked a stall and repeated the exercise from two days before.

Ushers at an arena generally patrol and assist the same areas every night. Now that he was on the other side of the arena, Al knew there was little chance that he would encounter the same usher. It was crucial to avoid the first usher in order not to raise suspicion. Surely the staff would wonder why this senior citizen kept finding lights that were out! He found a different usher and once again reported a light malfunction out of concern for his and others' safety. He waited within view of the bathroom entrance. Bingo. The man entering the stall this time was quite a bit younger. He carried a long florescent bulb with him but no toolbox. He was a part-time weekend worker for sure. Al also noticed something else. He was most likely a student. It was the shoes.

During his time teaching at the university, Al had noticed that no matter how the young men were dressed, designer sneakers were an essential part of their wardrobe. Leaving class one morning he had seen a young man with a very interesting pair of sneakers. They were burnt orange in color with the company logo embroidered on the side. He had jokingly said to the student, "Nice shoes. My goodness those must have cost a hundred and fifty dollars."

The young man had burst into laughter and replied, "How about two seventy five?"

Stunned, Al's face had betrayed the depth of his shock. He was out of touch. He remembered his childhood PF Flyers for $3.99. The rich kids wore Converse All Stars for $11.99. Al remembered wondering how anybody could pay nearly twelve dollars for a pair of sneakers.

The shoes the young and inexperienced repairman wore were multi-colored. They started out black on the lower portion and gradually transformed into a reddish orange near the top. A space-age, engineered sole capped off the construction which, for a final flourish, incorporated an intricately tied red and black shoelace combination. He had to be a student. He was working part time but had to make sure his appearance on the campus was up to snuff. Al's plan would work perfectly this time.

Since the young man had only brought a bulb, the stall remained dark when he left. That suited Al just fine. He tailed the repairman back to the hangout for the maintenance workers. A little alcove off of section 126. The professor would make his way back there as the show was nearing its end, imagining he would not have to wait very long for his target after the show. The young man would want to get out fairly quickly. As the show ended, Al pretended to be looking for a lost item. All of the vending areas were now caged and locked so eating a snack while loitering was not an option. As the concourse was just about clear, he saw sneaker guy come out of the shack. Al smiled to himself. He'd been right about the timing. The young man was wearing the bright red jacket of the maintenance crew, and a ring of keys could be heard jingling in the jacket pocket.

Careful not to seem suspicious, Al followed the young man out of the arena. He was even surer now that his target only worked part-time because he didn't even have underground parking privileges. Al slowly closed the gap between them as they reached the parking lot. Just as the young man placed the key in the door of the worn down Nissan, Al spoke to him.

"Good evening. Time to get home and study now?"

Startled, Sneakers looked up. "Do I know you?"

"No, I'm just guessing you are a student. Part-time job here at the arena trying to get that God-awful tuition paid, right? What's your major?"

Disarmed by the friendly old man, the student said, "Journalism. I'm going to be a sportswriter."

"That's great! I used to teach at the university. Are you close to finishing?"

"Two more semesters but … well …" Sneakers looked down, trying to evade Al's curiosity. "The money is running low."

In all their years of fishing together, CC had taught Al never to pull too quickly on the line so as not to yank the hook right out. He eased off. "Well you have a good night. Maybe I will one day read your articles." Walking past Sneakers, Al paused and pretended to be confused about where his car was located. "Damn!"

"Is something wrong sir?"

"I always forget where I park. I think I came out on the wrong side of the arena."

"I would be happy to drive you there. It's probably not the best idea for you to walk there by yourself. It's getting a bit late."

"I wouldn't want to put you out," Al protested.

"Oh, it's no trouble."

Al had a disarming appearance. His students often fell prey to the facade of the kindly professor only to discover that he would flunk them out in a minute. "Well if you really don't mind," Al said.

"Just a minute while I clear the front seat." The young man opened the passenger side door and began to shovel loads of paper, empty water bottles, and snack wrappers into the back seat. Al noticed that of all the things the kid had shoved onto the back seat, there was no mask among the items. These idiots just didn't get it. After Sneakers had brushed crumbs off the front seat, he invited Al to get in.

Once they had driven across two parking lots, Al spotted his car. "Oh this is it. Right over there. Thank you so much." Then Al inquired, "What's your name?"

"My friends call me Swiss. Not 'cause I'm from Switzerland, but because that's the kind of cheese I put on all my sandwiches."

"I'm Frank," Al replied. Then he opened the passenger door and stepped out. "Say, Swiss, how would like to make some money?"

Swiss turned his head toward Al but did not speak.

Serious now, Al said very evenly, "I don't play a lot of games, but if you give me your jacket and keys from the arena, I will give you two thousand dollars."

Swiss burst into laughter.

Al's face did not change. "There is no job you could get that will pay you two thousand dollars for such little effort."

"What do you need my jacket and keys for?"

Al took the two stacks of fifties out of his pocket. It was chancy but Al had calculated the risk.

The younger man stared at Al and the two thousand dollars. "How do you know I won't just take it and leave?"

"Do you think I would be foolish enough to be out here all by myself? If you were to do that, you would never get to spend it." Al's voice hardened slightly.

"What if I just go back in and tell security someone just tried to buy my keys?"

"You could do that. Go and tell them that an old Black man on the parking lot just offered you two thousand dollars for your jacket and keys. Call me when they finish laughing. Look kid, I don't have all night. This is a one-time take it or leave it offer. If you leave it, I'll just find someone else."

Swiss looked at the money. Two thousand dollars would cut his tuition bill down to almost nothing. He imagined his mother watching him walk across the stage in his cap and gown. Then he stepped out of the car and peeled off his jacket, leaving the keys in the pocket. He handed them to Al, got in his car, and drove away.

Although Al had planned to duplicate an ID badge, he realized he didn't have to. Johnathan Francis had inadvertently left his ID badge in the pocket. The photo swap would be no challenge at all.

37

DESPITE HIS ACADEMIC BRILLIANCE, PROFESSOR MCGUIRE was all thumbs when it came to mechanical devices. Early in their marriage Marnie had discovered that simple wiring and simple repairs were too much for her husband's patience. A single heating element once burned out on their electric range, and Al insisted on repairing it himself rather than paying the forty-dollar fee for a service call. He purchased the correct burner from an appliance store and proceeded to begin the repair. About fifteen minutes into the job, the lights in the house dimmed and a loud pop came from the range top. Al had not considered that it might be a good idea to turn off the circuit before fixing the appliance. When Marnie called the service team for the now totally burned out stovetop, the fee was over four hundred dollars. Al did not attempt any further home repairs.

The book arrived in the usual Amazon packaging. Al was suspicious of the digital fingerprints that online searches created and felt a book would leave a lighter trail. The yellow and black cover read *HVAC for Dummies*. It was the perfect guide to the basic principles of heating and cooling systems. The book taught him the fundamentals but not the routine setup of large facilities. To keep his home computer clean, Al went to the parish library. He logged in to one of the online computers there and searched for the usual setup of large buildings and how their HVAC units were configured. All of the units were located on rooftops.

Back at the house, Al went straight to the section of the book he needed next: air distribution. It wasn't complicated at all. Air distribution was simply getting the warmed or cooled air to the areas that needed cooling or warming. To do that, there had to be a system of ducts to forward the conditioned air. No matter what types of units were on the roof of the Louisiana Sports Arena, he merely had to find a unit connecting large ducts and blowing air. Return air ducts, heater coils, boilers, and all the other components of the HVAC were irrelevant. He just needed the air distribution section. It is there he would make them all pay for what they had done to Marnie. As they sat cheering, screaming, half-drunk on refills of their wretched beer, they would breathe in the consequences of their wanton recklessness. They would be forced to partake of their total disregard for lives other than their own.

Al walked over to the HVAC unit for his own house, located outside the patio door and nestled in the shrubs. The intake fan hummed. He had often heard it click on and off in an effort to keep conditions livable. He located an access panel on the grayish ductwork leading away from the unit, kept closed by a simple thumb bolt. He immediately opened it, and air rushed past his hand. Then he walked back into the house and went into Marnie's dressing closet, finding it dusty but largely untouched. Marnie had been a perfumed powder fanatic. Al picked up the container of her favorite fragrance. Shaking a handful of the powder into his hand he walked back outside. He reached his hand inside the open access panel of the ductwork and slowly released the powder into the duct. After closing the panel, he walked back into the house. In a few seconds, Marnie was everywhere. The powder was invisible, but her scent filled the room. The fragrant particles, which had been a visible clump in Al's hand before he released them into the ductwork, were completely invisible to the naked eye as they circulated throughout the house. The powder could not be seen, but it still stimulated Al's olfactory nerves, bringing Marnie back to life.

The professor was well aware that the human eye cannot see a particle smaller than 50 microns, or 50 millionths of a meter. There would be no way to detect the viral "fragrance" he would release, whose particles were 250 times smaller than that. This deadly fragrance would secretly take up residence in the nose, mouth, and lungs of the cottonmouth vipers that had taken his Marnie. Within himself, Al quietly rejoiced.

"Inhale deeply boys, your time is almost here."

38

"CURVE FLATTENS" READ THE MAIN HEADLINE ON THE CITY'S flagship newspaper. The news of fewer new cases was welcome for business owners and politicians. But not only for them. As though released from Alcatraz after a thirty-year sentence, hordes flocked to bars and restaurants like nothing had ever happened. Since mask wearing had become a sign of weakness and fear to many, these large gatherings were largely unmasked. Lillian put down the waiting room newspaper and shook her head in disgust. It was true that the number of admissions to the intensive care unit had declined, but that was largely due to the measures put into place to slow the spread. Earlier that day, she and Tasha had lamented to one another in the ICU.

"It's a mess, doctor. You're standing in a rainstorm screaming about how wet you're getting. Then you put up an umbrella and the rain misses you. After a while you even start to dry a little. But the rain is still pouring. How stupid it is to put the umbrella down and say, 'Well, I'm getting dry now, so I don't need this umbrella anymore.' I just don't understand these people."

Lillian had nodded in resigned agreement, munching on her Granny Smith apple. Though simple, the analogy was totally accurate. She knew that in just a few weeks the numbers would ramp back up and there would once again be no end to the influx of the critically ill.

Lillian was also increasingly worried about her old friend. She hadn't seen him for weeks. She realized that she was just going to have to barge into his lab and make him sit down and talk to her. She couldn't do it that weekend because she was on call, but the next weekend she would. In the back of her mind Lillian wondered if Doc would actually succeed in devising a method to decrease the virulence of the virus. What a contribution that would be. A testament to his greatness and compassion.

The service technician came into the waiting area. "Ms. Manning? Your vehicle is ready. I gotta hand it to you, ma'am. It's in excellent shape. Like brand new. We were going to wash it, but it was already spotless."

Lillian smiled, thanked the tech, and turned to go to the cashier. She loved owning the Supra, but the downside was that even for routine procedures the maintenance was not cheap. She provided her card and then headed for her baby. During the short walk there, Lillian thought about her life. Did she wish that someone rode regularly in her passenger seat? Or that she rode in someone else's. No, dating could wait. She enjoyed her work and had a great career. Plus she could devote her minimal free time to the Supra and honing her driving skills. That wouldn't be possible if she were in a relationship. Frankly she enjoyed the freedom of being unattached, of not having to feel someone else's hurts and tragedies as her own. She felt a slight pang of guilt thinking about how unhappy the professor had to be. She realized she shouldn't wait until next weekend. Maybe she would drop by the lab this evening just to say hello.

She tapped on lightly on the door of the lab at the end of the hall. "Doc?"

There was no answer.

"Doc?" she said a little louder. "Are you in there? It's me Lil Man."

"Oh great," a voice answered from inside. "Give me one second."

Lillian wasn't sure but she thought she heard the unmistakable sound of papers rustling. What was there to hide in a research lab? Maybe he was just trying to tidy up?

"Okay, come in," the professor said. "I haven't seen you in forever." The two hugged.

She had missed the professor and hugged him tighter. She knew she was supposed to maintain social distancing practices, but he was practically her father. Plus they were both routinely conscientious and careful. So she took the risk, deciding it was negligible.

"What brings you here, Lil?" Al gently asked.

"I just missed you and wanted to stop by. How is the research coming?"

"Well, you know how research is. It's slow and steady but I am sure I will have some progress soon."

Just then the lab door swung open. "What's all the racket over here?" Dr. Bales cried out with a dry smile on his lips. "I see, Al! you are hiding a beautiful woman in here without telling me."

"Cliff, this is my very good friend and daughter, Lillian. Marnie and I practically adopted her when she started her residency here in town."

Lillian extended a hand. "Pleased to meet you, Cliff."

The two of them shook hands but Cliff held onto Lillian's just a microsecond too long.

"I was just stopping by to see my dad," Lillian said, emphasizing the filial nature of her relationship with Al. "I've been worried about him. I think he's working too hard."

"Oh, but it has paid off," Cliff countered. "Did you tell her?"

Lillian looked puzzled. "Tell me what?"

"Your dad has exchanged two base pairs from a herpetic gene into a Q47cx gene and may have just discovered a way to make the virus far less deadly!"

"Well, we still have a ways to go," Al offered sheepishly.

Lillian was flabbergasted. "Well that's wonderful! No wonder you've spent so much time here lately. That's just incredible!" She noticed Al growing increasingly uncomfortable and decided to discreetly bring the visit to an end. "Ok well I'm not going to stay; I have a lot to get done this evening. But it's nice to meet you Cliff. And Doc, I'll call you within the next week. We'll have dinner again."

She left the lab and headed toward her car.

Lillian had known Dr. McGuire long enough to know that something wasn't right. He was a terrible liar. Over the years she had pondered why and settled on the idea that those who search relentlessly for the truth have a hard time with deception. Whatever the reason, Lillian knew something was wrong. The professor had never been able to surprise Marnie with anything at all, let alone a surprise party, because she could tell instantly when he was lying. Once when Lillian asked how she could tell so easily, she had simply replied, "Caffeine." Lillian had no idea what that meant, and now that Marnie was gone, she would never know. But one thing was certain. There was something about the professor's research project that he was hiding.

39

WITH THE MEANS TO ENTER THE ARENA, AL STILL HAD MORE work to do. He found and visited a store that specialized in metrosexual attire and accessories, a notable accomplishment as such places were rare in the Deep South. He felt a little out of place entering the store because the majority of the shoppers were at least thirty years his junior. They all seemed to have a similar style. Looking closely at their trousers, Al wondered how they got their feet into them. The tight fit around the ankle would have certainly been a challenge for him.

The clerk approached him in a relatively cautious manner. "May I help you, sir?" He placed a slight emphasis on "you," as if to ask, "Why are you, an old man, here in the first place?"

"Yes," Al replied. "I am looking for ... I think they call it a man bag for my nephew."

The clerk immediately brightened as he now realized his suspicion was correct. The old man was not there for himself. "What did you have in mind?"

"Well, it has to be a little bigger than this size," Al said, pointing to a mannequin with a small shoulder bag slung on his shoulder, "but not that big," pointing to another bag on the shelf. "Preferably black, but a dark brown would do. Oh, and I will need one with a buckle. My nephew seems to like shiny buckles."

The clerk put up a finger and walked to the back of the store. He brought back three bags. Each was a dark color but only one had a large buckle on the front.

"I think that one will be fine," Al said smiling. He paid with cash, to the surprise and disdain of the cashier, and left the store.

After Al returned home, he removed all of the keys from the key ring he had bought from the young man, Swiss. Carefully calibrating the settings on his 3D printer, he duplicated each key. The polycarbonate keys were just as hard as the originals, but the metal detector at the arena would be blind to them. Just to make sure his technique worked, Al took his own house key and printed a duplicate. He then locked his front door. The polycarbonate key easily opened the lock. It was crucial that the duplicates worked perfectly or the whole exercise would fail.

There were sixteen keys laying next to the printer now, eight originals and eight duplicates. Al didn't know if there was a master key among them or if all of the keys fit individual locks. He was certain there would be a key to the roof, where he needed to be. Then he took the eight duplicates to a small desk in what used to be a sewing room. Through the years it had basically become an all-purpose room because Marnie rarely sewed. He laid the keys out and collected his newly purchased man bag. Opening the bag, he very carefully cut the lining along the seam. He taped each individual duplicate to the bottom of the bag so that the keys did not clatter against each other. Even though they would not be detected as metal objects, he did not want items clanking in the bottom of the bag. When the keys were taped in, he carefully glued the edges of the lining back down. Allowing it to dry, he inspected his work. The cut was virtually invisible.

Professor McGuire removed what had been a storage drawer from the old sewing table and retrieved a calendar and a circular. A date was circled and marked on the calendar. The date circled only said "Marnie's

Day." He placed the circular next to the calendar. The brightly colored notice displayed a list of the events planned for the newly re-opened arena. Al regularly checked the arena's ticketing website, and as of that morning the events were booked up to three-quarters capacity. He once again wondered about how they would keep the crowds apart. Then he realized that on Marnie's Day, it wouldn't really matter.

The date marked on the colorful circular was September 20th. A Saturday night. It was the huge regional competition of the CMAA, the Combination Martial Arts Association. Thousands of testosterone-intoxicated young men and some young women would gather at the Louisiana Sports Arena that night to watch a couple of dozen of their equally macho peers beat the daylights out of each other. Knees to the face and elbows to the back of the head would bring howls of enjoyment. Eventually one fighter would manage to place his locked arm around the throat of his competitor, compressing the carotid artery's circulation long enough for the victim to pass out. If he was lucky, he would have enough of his faculties left to tap the floor to be released before he lost consciousness. In the crowd, beer would flow, and each attendee would leave the arena feeling just a little bit more manly than before he arrived. Al had always thought it was a shame that debates and college bowls did not draw a crowd. Academic achievement could be lifted up as an ideal, but at the end of the day most people just wanted to see violence. What a society.

With his preparation at home nearly completed, Al returned to his lab. He had taken the time to meticulously lyophilize the cell cultures containing the poison he would deliver to Marnie's killers. The elegant simplicity of lyophilization had always appealed to Al, ever since he had been a high school student. It was a sophisticated process of freeze-drying that made the storage and transport of perishable materials much easier. As a young man sitting in his school library, Al had been in awe that you could just freeze a sample, make some pressure and temperature adjustments, and then remove the water from that sample. Then you would have a final product with a much smaller volume so that it could be easily transported. Using this method, the now grieving widower had been able to reduce millions of viral particles to a volume small enough to fit in a small pressurized vial. The challenge would be getting the vial past the security scanners because a metal top was necessary to hold its contents under pressure. But Al had already solved that problem.

When the time came, Al once again slit the lining of the man bag. But this time the very small slit was just below the buckle on the bag. The buckle was not for decoration as the salesman had assumed. The buckle was there to purposely set off the metal detector. At the entry point they would carefully search the bag and find nothing. They would then scan buckle and see that it was triggering the alarm. The bag would pass without further inspection.

Once inside the arena Al's real work would begin. Once he had released the virus, the attack on the sports fans' immune systems would be closely followed by the raving symptoms of respiratory difficulty and sensations of suffocation. Unlike the barbaric competitors in the ring, they would not be able to tap out. Their significant others, protected by their higher levels of estrogen, would only be able to watch their men deteriorate on iPad screens from outside intensive care units packed to capacity. Those men would die alone. Just like Marnie. Alone.

40

SOMETHING WAS WRONG. SHE COULDN'T PUT A FINGER ON IT, but something was just wrong. The nagging thought would not leave Lillian alone. She sat picking at her late lunch across from Stacey, a wonderful ER nurse who had really been there for her during her grueling first year of residency. But Lillian had no appetite for the wilted romaine leaves heavy under the weight of olive oil dressing. Something was wrong. She decided to confide in her friend, who insisted Lillian explain what was bothering her. Lillian recounted the entire story—careful to omit any incriminating parts—and told Stacey that the professor had been working on a research project since Marnie's death but otherwise seemed depressed, absent, and evasive.

"I don't know. I just have a bad feeling."

"Girl, it doesn't sound that deep to me. Just an elderly man burying himself in work to escape his grief. Why not be glad he's active instead of following Marnie to the grave, like so many widowers do?"

"I know. At first I was happy for him. But seeing him at the lab the other day … Something was just … off."

"Well if it would make you feel better, why not drop in on him?"

Stacey was right. That evening she would go back to check on Doc and insist he talk to her.

As their lunch continued, Stacey and Lillian quietly discussed how everyone at the hospital, whether physician, nurse, respiratory therapist, or housekeeper, was approaching their breaking point, if they hadn't passed it already. There seemed to be an omnipresent pall of doom. Suddenly, Lillian brightened.

"You know, Stacey, I just realized I have a couple of hours to myself."

"Me too! And my house is empty. Darius is working the late shift and his mother is watching Nathan and Gabrielle. Come back to my place for a movie?"

"Yes, girl. Anything funny and mindless. I'm in."

They drove separate cars to Stacey's. The days were shorter now, so twilight was approaching. There was an uncommon coolness in the fall air and Lillian clutched the neck of her jogging suit a little tighter. The suit matched the red of her "baby" quite well. As she got into the Supra, she suddenly stopped. A piece of vegetative debris, maybe a portion of a leaf or a twig fragment had landed on her hood. She went to the hood of her car and carefully blew it off. Success! Spotless! Maybe she couldn't do anything about Doc's pain and grief, but at least her beloved Supra was pristine.

By 7:30 p.m., Katniss Everdeen had done her thing with bow and arrows, and a few more of the chosen had been eliminated. Lillian and Stacey had watched two features of *The Hunger Games* and promised each other that they would finish the entire series another time. Even though the films had been released years before, Lillian hadn't seen them. Of course not. Residency was grueling, and whenever she had free time, she usually spent it in the Supra or with Doc and M&M, not in a movie theater. But it had been so good to sit with Stacey in front of the flatscreen TV and disappear into another reality for a few hours. Lillian felt grateful for her first real moments of relaxation since Marnie's death. The two hugged and vowed to see each other more in the next couple of months. But each woman guessed it probably wouldn't happen. They both knew from experience that good friends are an asset in stressful times but, past a certain point, friendships can add stress. Right now, Lillian and Stacey could enjoy a couple of good movies together but felt no need to send each other birthday cards or party invitations. Neither of them had any obligation to cook meals or make extra car trips if calamity befell the other. They were both satisfied with the relationship as it was.

Lillian got into her car and mentally plotted a course home. She would try the house first and if the professor was not there she would go directly to the lab. She had to know what seemed to be bothering him and why he was evasive. Usually preferring to drive with the windows and the sunroof open, Lillian noted that this evening was a little too cool for that. She put the windows up and turned on the rarely used climate-control system. The upside was that she could hear the sound system much more clearly. She and Beyoncé made their way toward Al.

41

BY SIX O'CLOCK SATURDAY EVENING, AL WAS SET TO GO. The cool weather provided a perfect cover for his attire. He had zipped the bulky hooded sweatshirt with the university logo nearly to the top to hide the arena maintenance jacket beneath it. Non-descript dark pants completed his makeshift uniform. On his feet he wore a pair of work boots, similar in style to those of the first worker he had seen while doing his reconnaissance. His stylish man bag carried the polycarbonate keys and a neatly concealed vial of the deadly virus. Because the vial was pressurized, if the seal was broken or the glass cracked, it would immediately create a tiny explosion and circulate the contents of the vial further than if it were just passively dropped. To make the bag appear authentic, Al dropped in a few more items. He added a comb, a notepad, a package of hand sanitizer, and tissues. He shook the bag. The keys were secure.

Al decided he would not take his car. If anything went awry and there was a search, one of the first things the authorities would do was search and investigate as many of the cars on the lot as they could. Al looked at the ride sharing app on his phone but decided not to use it. Ride sharing drivers tended to be personable and therefore more likely to remember who they took where. In addition, there would be a documented transaction on his credit card statement. Al called an old-fashioned taxi.

Upon the arrival of the taxi, Al opened the back door and stated his destination: the Hamilton Hotel. There was no need for him to be dropped off at the arena. The Hamilton was three blocks away and a frequent stop for visiting athletes and spectators. It didn't matter if it was full or not. He would not be checking into a room.

"Kinda cool tonight, ain't it?" the taxi driver asked.

"Yep sure is." Al's monotone was the universal signal for requesting a silent ride.

The driver obliged. When they arrived at The Hamilton, Al exited and tipped the driver for the fare. He was careful not to make the tip too large or too small, as either would create a unique memory.

He made his way to the ticket window and purchased one ticket. During the transaction he made a small fuss about where his seat would be in order to convince any onlookers that he had not come for any other reason but to see the event. As it turned out, the planning for the man bag had not really been necessary. This time at the checkpoint, the singing, flirting, disinterested kid paid little attention to Al. The professor placed the bag on the table, and the distracted attendant opened it up. He moved his head back and forth pretending to look inside, then shone a light in it. At that point he looked away at one of the young women attendants, just before handing the bag back to Al. The professor chuckled to himself. He could have had a sub-machine gun in the bag and the kid would never have noticed. He was in. Though it was still early, the crowd was forming and already getting raucous. Vendors hawked beer on the concourse, and once again the smell of popcorn was in the air.

Downloaded onto Al's phone was a schematic of the arena. His seat was in section 314. In popular vernacular it was the nosebleed section. That was exactly where he wanted to sit. The closer to the roof the better. The crowd would be in and out during the first set of fights, but the majority would be in their seats for the final matches. Those fighters would be the well-known names the spectators had come to see, and their headline matches would begin around nine o'clock. Al found his aisle seat and waited. It was amazing anyone could see from this far up. The fighters were tiny specks against the pale colored ring. If he had really been interested, it would have been a spectacular waste of money.

Taking out his phone, Al surveyed his position. He was in the upper deck near the west end. There was a blank section near the north end. Al surmised that roof access would likely be there. As the pugilists and street fighters pummeled each other and the crowd roared, Al left his seat to go the nearest restroom. He entered a stall and promptly began removing his hooded sweatshirt. He smoothed the vest jacket underneath and pinned Swiss's ID badge to the front pocket. The original name and the barcode were displayed, but Al had carefully replaced the picture with his own. There were a large number of workers with many different areas to manage and patrol. It was unlikely anyone would think he was out of place.

How ironic it was. Dressed illegally as a maintenance man, he would be able to walk anywhere he wanted in the arena without being questioned. He remembered being invited to a retirement party for one of his former colleagues a few years back. After arriving at the country club, he had dropped Marnie off at the door. The parking area was a good distance away and he did not want her to walk. In his tuxedo he was stopped twice before he reached the entrance to the ballroom. Black man dressed in a maintenance outfit about to kill an arena full of folks, fine. Black man dressed in a tuxedo going to a country club ball, highly suspicious. Al shook his head. He would likely have no problem reaching the roof.

42

LILLIAN ARRIVED AT THE HOUSE JUST AFTER EIGHT O'CLOCK.
She was surprised to see both cars. Since she had figured Al would still be at
the lab, she had only expected to see Marnie's car in the driveway. Al almost
never drove it. Even when Marnie was alive, he kept it gassed up for her but
would not drive it. Lillian still remembered the day she'd asked him why.

"You know Lil Man, I can never get the seat exactly back in the right
place where she wants it. So I just don't tempt fate. Besides, it's too
small! I just fill it up with the gas can, so she can always go where she
wants to."

The memory of Doc's tenderness toward M&M made Lillian glad
she'd taken Stacey's advice to go see him. She moved through the back
decontamination area where she usually entered the house, but this time
she did not stop. She had not been on duty and was careful not to
touch anything in the area that could still have carried a trace of the
virus. Then she moved down the hall into the kitchen area. Something
was strange about the house. Light streamed from the door where Al
and Marnie's bedroom was located. "Dr. McGuire," Lillian called out.
No answer. "Doc?" she called out even louder this time. No answer.
Suddenly she feared the worst, that the angina had progressed into a

full-blown heart attack. She was sure when she rounded the corner that she would find him sprawled out on the bed. She hurried to the door and knocked firmly. "Professor McGuire?" There was no answer. She slowly pushed the door open and peered inside.

The room was a mess. Papers were strewn all over the bed and a good portion of the floor. The bed was unmade but looked like it had not been slept in for weeks, or even months. The pillows were askew, and the comforter lay on the floor at the foot of the bed. The light Lillian had seen under the door emanated from a table lamp next to the bed. Near the lamp, on the far side of the bed, she saw the tip of a small red cloth poking out from under a pillow. Then she called out once more quite loudly, "Doc!"

Still no answer. Lillian slowly approached the bed. She felt like an intruder, but she needed to know what was going on. Was Doc okay? As she neared the bed, she recognized the flash of red underneath the pillow. It was the scarf Marnie used each night to tie up her thinning hair. Apparently, it had not been moved since she had gone to the hospital.

Curious now, Lillian took a step closer to better examine the papers on the bed. Diagrams and structures of various chemical formulas depicted variations in genomic base pairs. Clearly it was a part of the professor's work. But why was it here and not in the lab? Before Marnie's death, Lillian had never known Dr. McGuire to do intense intellectual work at the house. Besides he was rarely at home except when she wasn't. Was that by design? Was that so he wouldn't have to talk to her? She continued to scan the surface of the bed, looking over the papers for any kind of clue. Then her eyes rested on something that sent a cold shock through her. On the far right corner of the bed was a calendar. The kind of calendar given to insurance clients, the spiral type that usually hangs on a wall. Circled in heavy black ink on the calendar was a date. Today's date.

An arrow pointed to the circled date with the words "Marnie's Day" next to the arrow. Lillian was puzzled because Marnie's birthday was months away. She lifted the calendar off the bed to get a closer look. As she did, a small circular fell from between the pages. It was a handbill advertising an event at the Louisiana Sports Arena. A handwritten star appeared on the circular, just above a full-color picture of a fighter in a full flying spin-hook kick nearing the face of his opponent. The date on the flyer was today's date.

Under the lamp next to what would have been the professor's side of the bed was another folded piece of paper. A diagram of a commercial HVAC system was marked and noted. Things were finally starting to make sense. Lillian was not sure exactly what it was, but Dr. McGuire was planning something for the event that was happening today at the arena. Whatever he was planning had to do with the HVAC system. She knew of his growing disdain for young people, especially young men, following Marnie's death. She knew he held them responsible for her illness. The diagram fell from Lillian's hand. His furtive, embarrassed looks in the lab that day with Dr. Bales suddenly made sense. As did the quiet agitation she had sensed when he had asked her to get him a sample of the virus. She heard the professor's words ringing in her ears. "I am going to find a whole new approach to fighting this plague. I am going to dedicate my discoveries to Marnie's memory. I am going to genetically alter the virus' RNA."

Lillian involuntarily let out a small gasp. Al had planned something to avenge Marnie's death. Something unthinkable. She had to get there. She had to stop him. If she failed, not only would countless lives be lost but his brilliant career would be permanently overshadowed by an act of terrorism.

Lillian pulled her phone from her pocket and checked the time. It was 8:22. The event started at 8:00. She could only pray that she would get there before it was too late and somehow find the professor. She rang his phone. No answer. She knew there wouldn't be. Time was running out. She deduced that he had taken some other form of transportation into the arena because he did not want his car there.

ERIC A. YANCY, MD

Bad sign. There was only one chance to save the professor and maybe thousands of lives. Get there.

As Lillian considered her next steps, she drew a slow, deep breath. She reminded herself, as she did during punishing moments at the hospital, that the human mind cannot concentrate on two things at one time. What it *can* do is move rapidly between any number of thoughts with such speed that the result seems to be simultaneous concentration. For years, Lillian had honed that skill, not only as a doctor but also as a driver, racing at impossible speeds on the go-kart track. Reminding herself that she had trained for this moment did successfully slow her heart rate down, but the panic and grief in her belly did not budge.

The sensation transported her back in time, to the day after she had lost her gold locket, a gift from her mother. Lillian had been nine or ten, crying inconsolably in Sunday School. Her teacher, a very old, very wise woman named Miss Elnora, had said, "It's ok, baby, we don' always know, but God do evahthang fuh a reason." Lillian thought of the Supra on the driveway and knew what she was there to do.

She felt for the key fob in her pocket and pulled it out. She double clicked the circular image on the fob and she faintly heard two beeps of the horn and the engine roar to life. Her remote starter had done the trick. She ran out of the house through the garage, not bothering with the alarm. Reaching the garage, she frantically searched the tool rack. She found it. A rather large five-pound ball peen hammer. Al had used it to break up stones to line the driveway. It was just right. Once outside, she closed the garage door by placing her hand inside and pushing the button on the wall. She snatched her hand out before it could break the beam sensor that would send the door back up.

As Lillian approached the powerful Supra, its lights were already on. The cool evening made visible thin puffs of vapor coming from the twin tailpipes. She surveyed her baby and without hesitation took the large hammer and swung it at the rear of the car. Over and over she smashed the heavy hammer into the vehicle. Shards of glass flew and fell to the ground. Sweating and breathing heavily, Lillian dropped the tool and assessed her work. The back of the Supra was now totally dark. The top speed of the car was 155 mph with 0 to 60 in 4.1 seconds. She knew she would need its full capabilities in order to put a stop to whatever the professor had in mind. She couldn't be pulled over. The delay would be fatal for too many. Under her breath she whispered, "The cops can't follow what the cops can't see."

43

AL TOOK HIS FIRST LEISURELY WALK AROUND THE UPPER concourse with no hassle. Approximately halfway around the upper deck he found what he was looking for, a heavy metal door marked AUTHORIZED PERSONNEL ONLY. It was the door to the arena's work area. There would be people present but each would be totally focused on the event and unlikely to question him. He took out his keys and started to try them one by one. Fabricated key number four turned the tumblers. A couple of patrons wandered by but barely even gave Al a glance. His bright vest proved he was supposed to be there.

He stepped into an industrially lit hallway, spied a clipboard sitting on a table, and picked it up. Pretending to be inspecting a cable in the ceiling, he followed the corridor along, looking up. Looking up not only made him seem official but also helped him avoid eye contact. He knew he was a terrible liar. He began singing to himself, loudly enough to be heard by someone passing by. Surely a man bold enough to attract attention to himself by singing belonged there. His peripheral vision detected something worthy of examination. The yellow and black outline around the steel ladder told Al he had reached his destination. He tapped his pocket. The pressurized glass vial was still intact. He laid the clipboard against the wall and grabbed the first rung of the ladder.

Though his build was lean and athletic, Al's slightly asymmetric leg, age, and heart condition all slowed him down. The climb up the steep stairs was grueling. Fortunately, after the first ten steps the ladder led into a cylindrical structure so that the ladder appeared to end blindly into the ceiling. Once he reached that blind area, he could slow down a little. He clung to the ladder with all of his strength. A tiny pain started to creep into his chest. Al ignored it and kept climbing. After several more steps the pain increased. Instinctively, as he had done for a number of years, Al reached for his pills. He froze and drew a sharp breath. His fingertips felt only fabric where the rectangular tin should have been. Completely absorbed in his preparation for the arena event, he had left his pills on the table at home. He would just have to fight through his discomfort. Al climbed some more. *How high is this roof and how long is this ladder?* he thought. Sweating and dangerously tired now, he thought he could make out the dim markings of a hatch-like door. He slowly pulled himself up rung by rung. Yes it was another door. But it was locked.

Al shifted his weight to one side so he could reach into his pocket and take out the keys. This time, key number three did the job. He turned the lock and pushed on the heavy door. A light broke through. The hatch led into a small anteroom. Only one more door between him and the roof. With extraordinary effort, Al pulled himself into the anteroom. His chest now felt like a hundred-pound rock was sitting on it. Profusely sweating, he lay on the floor of the empty room. His pain was soaring to new levels now. He could feel it creeping down his left arm and into his neck. He needed his pills. Why had he forgotten his damned pills? Al struggled to breathe. He decided to just lie still, convinced it would pass.

44

LILLIAN'S FIRST ENCOUNTER WITH THE AUTHORITIES OCCURRED about four miles from the house. As the other car's headlights approached her from the opposite direction, there was no way for her to tell who was behind the wheel. It happened to be one of the parish deputy sheriffs. Lillian passed the car with such velocity that the deputy's car shook. He slammed on his brakes and turned around. Lillian immediately saw the lights atop the vehicle switch on. Ten seconds later the lights went back out. The deputy had looked and seen no taillights. At those speeds and with nothing to follow, he knew the chase would be futile. He just turned his car around and decided to finish his rounds. Meanwhile, Lillian kept herself calm and focused by turning up her sound system. Kendrick Lamar blared from every speaker and took her further toward her destination.

The Supra's second encounter with the police was more challenging, even though Lillian had almost been expecting it. After evading the first patrol car, she remembered that a few parishes had borrowed vehicles from the State Police for speed traps. She was aware that "trap" was a misnomer in her case, as she deserved every ticket they could give her. But there was just no time to slow down. Dr. McGuire had to be found and stopped. It was about 8:55 when Lillian passed a turnaround covered with overgrowth. Just as she suspected, it was a perfect hiding spot for police radar. Astounded, the trooper on the back country road saw the speed gun measure 116 miles per hour. With its engine already running, the black Camaro spun its tires, and the officer gave chase to the red missile that had just passed his post. The Camaro, with its 6.2 Liter LT1 V8 engine boasting 455 horses, could match the Supra no problem. But the Supra had one thing the Camaro didn't—a driver who knew every turnoff and back road like the proverbial back of her hand.

With no taillights to follow, the cop focused on the side glare made by Lillian's headlights. On the straights he was closing fast. Lillian knew that in less than a mile a curve would appear, followed by a farm road at a sharp turn. She just needed to put a little distance between the Supra and the police car. The trooper could not predict when she would brake because she had destroyed her brake lights. The Supra sped up as it approached the curve, but the Camaro was still closing in. Lillian braked hard at the curve and the trooper did just as she expected. Her surprise maneuver forced him to slam on his brakes at the very last minute, which took the Camaro—a vehicle with rear wheel drive—sideways and slightly off the road. The spin placed him not quite in the opposite direction but clearly facing away from his target. Lillian then punched the gas, accelerating quickly while rounding the curve. As the Camaro momentarily disappeared, she whipped into the side road and killed her lights. Thinking he had just lost her in front of him, the trooper shot forward out of the curve. Lillian watched as he sped past her on the open highway. She waited a full minute then crept back onto the highway, gradually bringing the Supra back up to speed. Vintage Tupac took her the rest of the way into town.

Lillian was sure that an all-points bulletin for her had already been issued. She knew from coffee-break conversations with EMTs that law enforcement agents took it as a personal affront if they were outrun by a civilian vehicle. Sure, legislators in municipalities all over the country had created "no chase" laws because of the threat posed to innocent bystanders. But those policies had little effect on officers' behavior. They continued to severely punish anyone apprehended in a high-speed pursuit, although they usually left the beatings out of their official reports. Getting caught and assaulted by the police was not an option for Lillian right now. She needed to find the professor.

The Supra blew into town and headed straight for the Louisiana Sports Arena. Lillian pulled into an area behind the arena in an alley. The alley was a known hangout spot for the homeless. But Lillian had never been put out by the homeless. She knew that many of them had been productive workers or homeowners and were just down on their luck. The virus had devastated their community. That was a part of its cruelty. The ones already disenfranchised were punished even further. As Lillian got out of her car, she noticed that the cool evening had driven the homeless to put out the barrels.

The city had frowned on the habit, but the homeless often used steel drums from the oil refinery to burn trash, wood scraps, or whatever fuel they could find. They would huddle around the barrels to keep warm on colder nights. Sometimes on warmer nights, they would just watch the fire, pretending they were camping. Lillian pulled past the last barrel. Yes, her car was a target but she couldn't keep it hidden and also do what was required to stop the professor. She made her way around to the front of the arena. The last ticket booth was about to close. She ran to the booth so fast that once she got there she was gasping for air. Breathlessly, she said, "One for the upper deck please."

45

AL WAS ALSO BREATHLESS BUT HANGING ON. TWICE NOW HE
had tried and failed to move. The rooftop was just a few feet away, but
he could not get there. He reached inside his pocket and clutched the
pressurized vial. Just a few more feet, he told himself, willing his limbs
to move. He could hear the hum of the gigantic fans cycling on and off
even through the wall. He let out a desperate wail as he tried one last
time to advance. But he had exhausted all his strength. He was drenched
in sweat, unable to budge.

Once inside the arena, Lillian knew where to look. The drawings
on the professor's bed had shown diagrams of heating and air condi-
tioning systems. In a building so huge there was only one place for
them to be. The roof. If Dr. McGuire were here, he would be trying
to make his way to the roof. Lillian ran around the upper bowl of the
arena, ignoring the stares of several spectators. She saw a large metal
door marked AUTHORIZED PERSONNEL ONLY. It had to be the
way to the roof. She tried the handle, but it was locked. She couldn't
just knock on the door and ask, "Have you seen an older gentleman
about to blow up the arena?" She would be instantly arrested. Lillian
had to think.

She ran to the concession stand and caught the staff just as they were about to put down the grate for the night.

"Wait!" she shouted. "I need some drinks."

"We already shut the machines off," the disinterested older woman said.

"Please," Lillian implored. "How about just eight cups of water with lids." The woman frowned as Lillian pulled out a fifty-dollar bill and a twenty. She laid them on the counter.

The woman behind the counter looked warily both ways and said, "Just a minute." She scooped up the money and returned with eight cups filled with ice water. She never turned the register back on. The cups were placed in two carriers, four in each one.

Lillian picked up the carriers and headed back toward the large steel door. She saw that the crowd was in a frenzy, apparently delighted that one of the fighters had suffered a concussion and lay motionless on the floor. When she reached the door, she began to kick it. She kicked and kicked at the bottom of the door. Eventually the door opened, and an annoyed middle-aged man stood staring at her. Lillian went into her act.

"You asked me to go get all of this crap, and then ain't nobody here to let me in? I told them to be here when I got back or I would just pour this shit out. I ain't your damn maid. They shoulda got all of this stuff at intermission. Running all over the place like a fool looking for drinks."

The technician looked at Lillian in her feigned outrage and said, "I'm sorry I'm sorry." He pushed the door open for her.

"Did you ask for a drink too?"

Too afraid to say yes, the man mumbled, "No, it's okay."

Pretending she knew exactly where she was going, Lillian turned and went in the opposite direction from the tech. She was in. How many times had she gotten what she wanted just by being what people expected her to be? By acting like she knew her place? But she had no time now to ponder the indignities of society.

She made her way around the curved hallway, drinks in hand. Then she spotted the yellow and black caution paint on the floor surrounding a steel ladder. That had to be it. It had to be the ladder access to the roof. She ran back down the hall a few feet to leave the tray. A woman with a headset was coming her way. Lillian stiffened.

"What are you doing up here?"

"I know damn well you not asking me what I'm doing up here. I just drug this crap up the stairs to your call-in order like I'm some damn McDonald's and you asking me what am I doing here? I got a great idea. You take these drinks and you pass them out. They'll know who ordered what. So here!"

Threatened with the idea of having her position lowered to that of a server, the woman said, "No, no. It's ok. You go right ahead."

Lillian glared at her as she walked away. When the woman with the headset had disappeared around the corner, Lillian dropped the tray on a table and ran for the ladder. She heard voices approaching as she scaled the ladder, but Lillian was far too quick to be caught. She was into the coned part of the tube before anyone had a chance to see her. The ladder was easy work for Lillian, who possessed the tone and balance of a dancer. She reached the hatch and miraculously found the door unlocked. In his haste and pain, Al had forgotten to lock the door behind him. She pushed the door open and propelled herself into the anteroom. A pained grunt startled her and made her turn around. There was the professor, laying on the floor in a pool of perspiration, clutching his chest. Lillian knew what was wrong.

46

"DOC! DOC!" SHE SAID IN A PAINED WHISPER. "DOC, WHY? Why?" She rushed to the old man and held his hand.

Breathless and anguished, he spoke in short gasps. "They killed my Marnie."

"But what are you doing here? What are you doing here tonight?"

"They killed my Marnie. They couldn't even cover their filthy mouths when they spread that venom onto everything and everybody. She didn't have to die. We had trips to take. She had a garden. We just wanted to be together. They killed my Marnie."

Al could barely breathe, but the force of all his pent-up frustration pushed the words out. "She picked up that virus from the store. The can that somebody left the virus on." The tears rolled from Al's eyes. "She gave her life to them. She taught them. She cried about them. She stayed up all night worrying about them and they didn't care. They killed her anyway." The anguish in Al's eyes hardened into rage. "And now they are all going to die."

"No, Doc. Marnie wouldn't want it that way. You said it yourself. She lived for them. She loved them." They were both crying now. Huddled on the cold floor of an anteroom leading to the roof, they held onto one another and wept. Lillian had lost one some months ago, and now she was losing the second of the only parents she had known for a very long time. "No, Doc, she would not want you to hurt them. Tell me what you did. Tell me what you did!" Lil pleaded.

Al felt not only the pain in his body but also a war within his heart. He did not want to involve Lillian in any way, but he realized was not going to make it. Just then, his visual field went dark and he heard the rapacious hiss of a cottonmouth. His resolve strengthened. Al reached inside his pocket and took out the vial.

"Lil Man, this contains a strain of virus that is more deadly than anything they have seen. It is spliced with base pairs that wipe out the adrenals."

Lillian looked at him, wondering if he had lost the ability to be coherent.

Al shook his head. "When the adrenal glands cease to function, the young men's ability to produce estrogen will be gone." Then he managed a grim smile. "After all they don't have ovaries. Their deaths will be fast and painful. Their wives and girlfriends will watch them suffer and die just like I watched my Marnie." Al handed her the vial. "Just take it and drop it into the first blower. It's right outside on the roof. We're only a few yards away. Lil, you have to do this for M&M." He gripped her arm with most his remaining strength.

Lillian stared at Al for a long time. She knew he thought she could carry out his plan and walk away scot-free, like she'd gotten him in to see Marnie at the hospital, like she'd gotten him a sample of the virus. Doc's whole life had revolved around Marnie. Some might say he loved her too much. But how could there be such a thing as too much love? Lillian's confusion was interrupted by a desperate wheeze.

"Take it," Al said. "You have to do this for her. For me."

Lillian's gaze met Al's. She saw the depths of his suffering. "I will, Doc. I will."

She felt his grip loosen. His eyes rolled back, a deep gurgle came from his throat, signifying his last breath, and he slipped away. Lillian cradled the professor's head in her lap as tears streamed down her face.

She wailed with her voice muffled against the top of his head. She shook with sobs. Then she took the vial. She knew what had to be done. She knew Doc was right. They had killed Marnie. Killed her with negligence and callousness. To them, she had just been one more old woman. Who really cared about Marnie? Who would rectify the injustice of her death?

Lillian clutched the vial in her hand. She decided to do what she knew Marnie would want. Her surrogate mother, who had given her entire life to the children of a broken society, would want something in return for all of her efforts. Lillian stood up and looked down at her friend. She stooped and straightened his jacket. She knelt, took the corner of her sleeve and wiped his eyes. The morning crew would find him and wonder how an old man had found his way to the roof of the arena. The circumstances of the professor's death broke Lillian's heart. His work had been largely ignored by the scientific establishment, so he had never received the national science awards he deserved. As a final indignity, his crowning achievement had been reduced to a weapon of mass destruction.

Lillian stepped away and walked toward the door leading to the roof. She turned the knob, pushed it open, and stepped out into the cold. An unusually strong wind was blowing. She made her way to the mammoth unit humming with a huge fan attached. Ductwork led away from the unit. There were likely diffusers on the other end of the ductwork, diffusers that would carry the vengeance of a broken genius whose final acts had been driven not by inspiration but by rage.

Lillian thought of Marnie and what she would make of the day's surreal events. She thought of the joy she had seen in Marnie's face the first time she, at ten years old, had discovered a new word or the solution to a new math problem. She thought of the love that imbued Marnie's voice every time she had spoken to one of her students. She thought of all of the visits Marnie had made to students' homes and the books she had purchased for them with her own money. Yet, one of that generation had killed her. One of them had taken her care and compassion and flicked it away like a cigarette butt or an empty beer can. But Lillian also knew that Marnie would not have held it against them. She would have loved them and taught them anyway. And if she had been granted infinite years, she would have taught their children, and their children's children. Teaching wasn't what Marnie did. It was who she was.

Lillian took the vial out of her pocket and looked at the humming blower. She placed it back in her pocket and headed back into the ante-room. She tried not to look at Al, feeling she had somehow betrayed him. In her heart she knew that she had not. The arena staff would wonder how he managed to get near the roof and what he was doing there, but at least nothing would tarnish his legacy as a scientist and educator. With the deadly vial in her pocket, Lillian darted back down the steel stairs.

If she were caught exiting the cylinder that housed the ladder, she would be detained. She would be searched and the vial analyzed. The professor would be tarnished forever, and she would likely be labeled a terrorist and imprisoned for life. As she neared the point on the ladder where she could be seen, she realized that an entire group of people might well be standing beneath her. She had to find a way to discover what was happening inside that room. She could hear that the matches weren't quite over. But there was still no time to climb all the way back up the ladder and come down head first because she had to get out before the hallway was flooded with exiting staff. She had to see into the room beneath her.

Lillian turned her tiny body in the cylindrical housing. She was still concealed. Her back was now against the ladder. She pressed herself hard against the ladder and with remarkable flexibility brought her knees up to chest level. Then splaying her knees out, almost to a frog-like position, she brought her legs up into a complete jackknife within the confines of the ladder tube. With pure strength, she pushed her legs up the side of the cone, ending in a completely upside-down position. She now hung suspended with her hands and feet on separate rungs.

Like a cat, she inched herself head first down the ladder with the bulk of her body weight resting on her hands. The vial, zipped in her top pocket, was secure.

She reached the opening of tube, where the ladder could be seen. Her hands barely visible, she placed her weight on them and dipped down so that she could see into the corridor. It was clear. She hurried down hands-first and, once free of the cone, flipped onto the floor. The crowd was wailing and screaming inside the arena. The barbarism was still in progress. She had time to get out of there without destroying the professor's legacy or her own life.

47

"HEY MIKEY, HOW'S YOUR SECOND WEEK ON THE JOB? BETTER than the first?" Sergeant Frank Butterman sniggered, ribbing his baby-faced partner.

"Yeah, real funny Butt. I consider it a badge of honor that the guys fooled me into scrubbing the toilets. At least I got to clean up that dump of a precinct instead of doing something useless. What did they do to you when you joined the force, Butt? Had pranks even been invented back then?" Michael Carlton knew he had to give as good as he got, or he'd never earn his supervising officer's respect.

"Hey, watch your mouth, choirboy. It was eighteen years ago, and there aren't many guys around who still remember my first week. I know you've got FBI dreams, Mikey, but you're gonna have to compete with a bunch of college kids. Let's see if you're up to solving the case of Butt's rookie prank before you think about trying for the bureau." Butt let out a short detached laugh. "I know you were number four in your class at the academy, and they say you got that pornographic—"

"Photographic memory, Butt."

"Yeah that. So I guess you think you're pretty smart. But let's see if you can figure out what they did to old Butt during his first week on the force."

Michael felt relieved that he was on Butt's good side. Sergeant Frank Butterman could be cruel. Legend in the department had it that Butt got his nickname from an arrest during which he had beaten a shoplifter unconscious with the butt of his service weapon. An investigation later exonerated him of any wrongdoing, and he was back on the street with a clean record within weeks. Michael, staring straight head in the passenger seat, observed Butt in his peripheral vision, noting that he was visibly agitated. Butt's years on the street had made him paranoid, and he was a hothead, always looking for action. Michael had anticipated this ride with his superior officer ever since he had discovered that the sergeant always volunteered to have the rookies tag along with him. Young men, anyway. In his entire career Butt had never requested to supervise one female officer.

Michael knew his reserved demeanor and intelligence made him a target for men like Butt. He wondered if the sergeant knew why he hadn't finished first in his class. During use-of-force training, a veteran instructor had ridden him hard and given him mediocre marks. When Michael had hesitated to use lethal force during one exercise, the instructor had screamed, "You're gonna get yourself and maybe your partner killed, recruit. The post office is down the street! Go apply there!" Michael fired at the suspect much more quickly during the next exercise, but he wasn't sure how fast his reflexes would be on the street.

There were occasional car break-ins during arena events, so Michael and Butt were on the lookout for any illegal activity around the area. They turned the corner of the street adjacent to the arena.

"Man, I wish I was in there right now," Butt said. "Beatdown of the year, I guarantee it. I know some of our guys scored tickets."

Just then the radio crackled. Lillian had been right about the APB. The trooper she had outwitted had gotten close enough to the Supra for long enough to be able to detect its color, rear-end damage, and missing taillights. But he'd been unable to provide a description of a driver.

After a slow pass around the east end of the building, the two officers drove slowly past an alley behind the arena. Skid row. Butt decided not to turn down the alley, as there was nothing there but homeless people begging for a handout. They were almost out of the view of the alley when Michael spotted something.

"Wait, Sarge. Didn't the APB say they were looking for a red car with a damaged rear end? I think I saw something."

Butt rolled his eyes, convinced his subordinate was wrong, but he backed up and pointed the headlights of the cruiser down the alley. A small red car with a bashed in rear end sat less than a hundred feet down the alley. They looked more closely. Could be the car, Butt thought.

"Should we call it in?"

The sergeant shook his head. "No way. The chase started out of our jurisdiction. If we call it in now, they tell us to stand down and the state's here in five. We're just gonna sit here and wait."

Twenty minutes passed. The event seemed to be nearing its end because a few patrons were straggling out toward the parking lot. The police car edged back to avoid being seen. Michael and Butt were still able to surveil the target vehicle because the glow of the fires in the steel barrels cast an eerie yellow light into the alley. A petite woman dressed in a red athletic suit made her way through the alley in the direction of the vehicle. As she approached the red car, the faint glare of the head-lights, which were pointed away from the police car, flashed.

"Here we go."

Michael noticed that Butt's voice was tight, on edge.

Lillian had pressed the remote entry key to her vehicle. She was so exhausted from the ordeal she had just suffered that she had let her guard down. She never looked down the alley before entering it and didn't notice the police vehicle until it was too late. In her hand she still held the vial of the lethal viral agent. By the time she detected move-ment out of the corner of her eye, the two officers had already exited their vehicle with guns drawn.

"Stop right there, Missy, and don't move."

Lillian clutched the deadly vial in her hand a little tighter.

"Turn toward us real slow and put your hands in the air. If you don't do what I say, I will kill you."

Michael remained quiet but he could not stop himself from thinking about the language that Butt had just used, language that he and countless other police offers had been trained to use. "I will kill you." Not "I will shoot you" or "I will disable you" or "I will use deadly force." Every single time, the admonition ended the same way: "Or I will kill you."

Lillian did as she was ordered. She turned slowly toward the officers with her right hand still clutching the vial. Is this where it would all end, she wondered? No, certainly not. She was one tiny woman and the two officers just had to listen to reason. In her hand was enough deadly virus to wipe out half the city. The spread would not be nearly as efficient as if the vial had been thrown into the ventilation system, but the virus would spread nevertheless. Ground zero would be right there in the alley.

"My name is Sergeant Frank Butterman, and I'm ordering to you to drop whatever you are holding in your hand."

Lillian's mind raced. She couldn't drop what she was holding. There was no way. She had to explain. "Officer," she said, "I can't—"

"Shut up you little bitch and drop it or I will kill you."

Her eyes moved to the younger officer.

With a steadiness in his voice, Michael said, "What was that ma'am?"

Lillian felt herself exhale. The young man was trying to help her.

"Shut up, Carlton!" Butt bellowed. "I'm in charge here."

Though Michael kept his Glock 19 trained on her, Lillian saw his hands shake just a little. The fire in the steel barrel six feet away lit his face with a pale glow. She could clearly see his blue eyes. They held no malice.

Michael knew she was no threat. She was holding something in her hand, but it was obviously not a weapon. It was too small to be a grenade, so there would be no harm in hearing her out. He thought of approaching her, but he knew that would end his field training. He would be disciplined severely and likely placed on probation. His dream of advancement in law enforcement would die. His children would never get to see their dad graduate from Quantico. Michael held his tongue.

Seeing the younger policeman capitulate, Lillian started to panic. She looked at the officer with spluttering rage in his eyes. How she longed to just drop the vial as ordered. Within seconds the pressurized glass would shatter, and they would rush to subdue her. They would unwittingly infect themselves and their whole precinct. It would only take days for them to die, lying in her intensive care unit, choking on endotracheal tubes with lines and ducts extending from every hole in their bodies. Part of her wanted to see them choke on their own vile bravado. Lillian willed herself out of her vengeful fantasy. No, she would to try to explain herself one more time. She had to explain why she couldn't just drop the vial. Her eyes darted from officer to officer. The younger man's eyes held hope. What a perfect microcosm of society, Lillian thought: The one who will listen has no power, and the one with power will not listen.

Lillian knew she had only seconds left to make a decision. She knew she would live if she dropped the vial. But for every one hundred Buttermans, there was perhaps one Carlton who deserved to live. Could he make the others listen to reason? Lillian also sensed the terror of the homeless in the alley behind her, now huddled at the far end of the filthy passage. They deserved a chance to survive. Marnie would not want them to suffer a senseless death. Lillian opened her eyes. With resignation in her heart, she realized she would not leave the alley alive. She closed her eyes and compressed her final calculations into fractions of a second.

"This is your last warning. Drop what's in your hand or I will kill you."

Lillian took a deep breath. She had found her target. The barrel that the homeless used for warmth on this chilly night was still glowing. She didn't need an active flame. The vial would drop to the bottom. Though the heat and pressure would immediately shatter the vial, it would be shattered surrounded by, and cradled in, a bed of embers with a temperature of nine hundred degrees. The virus would instantly vaporize. It was her only chance. She had to drop the vial into the barrel just three feet away before the bullets destroyed her ability to move. If she turned quickly, she could make it. She could not outrun the bullets, but her momentum would carry her over the necessary distance.

Metamorphosing into the dancer her mother had wanted her to become, Lillian quickly pivoted to her left, bringing her right hand in front of her body. If she had been performing in a ballet, it would have been the perfect execution of a glissade en tournant. Out of the corner of her eye, she only saw one muzzle flash. The cop with the kind eyes never fired. The first round exited Butterman's Glock pistol at 1,246 feet per second. The muzzle flashed again and the second bullet hurtled toward Lillian at the same velocity. And again. And again. Just before the first round ripped through her shoulder, the vial flipped from Lillian's hand. She saw it hang on the edge of the barrel just for an instant, then fall harmlessly into the embers as the bullets continued to tear through her body.

While some rounds seared into delicate tissue and bone, others missed altogether. Lillian prayed that those would not find an unsuspecting child further down the alley. Then a twin pair of bullets found their mark. The first burned a hole through the fabric of her stylish red athletic suit. A millisecond later, on the same deadly trajectory, the second made its way through the small lacy bra, through the breast that would never nurse a child, and into the chest wall. Slowing now but opening its hollowed-out point, the bullet mushroomed and split Lillian's pericardial sac, tearing into the taut muscle of her heart. Lillian felt her awareness drifting outside her own body. It slowly dawned on her that it is often untrue that people are "killed instantly." A few moments lapse before the brain realizes that it will receive no more nourishment. A little time must pass for it to know that the body has not simply fainted.

As Lillian lay on the ground in the alley, her brain slowly becoming aware of the finality of the moment, the voices that she was hearing became muffled. She felt the chilly night become a little cooler. She heard someone yell "Call an ambulance!" as though the voice were a long distance away. Her nostrils registered the thick smell of cordite even in the outside air. Her brain, now drifting into an endless void, allowed her pupils to record the image of the sky. Staring straight ahead, her face moved ever so slightly as a small smile gently crossed her lips.

"M&M? Doc?" Her eyes drifted shut in sleep.

Epilogue

IT WAS MIDMORNING ON A BEAUTIFUL SPRING DAY. LILLIAN found herself standing in a garden full of impeccably manicured flowers with a bright clear sky above. As she took in the beauty of the scene and inhaled the aroma of the flowers, she heard her name. "Lillian," the voice called softly. Lillian turned around to see none other than M&M. Young and with a full head of hair, she was dressed in a pair of shorts and a brightly-colored blouse. Behind her, laughing and walking toward her, was the professor. He walked without a limp, and he, too, seemed the picture of health. "Why don't you have brunch with us?" Marnie said. Speechless, Lillian could not believe she was seeing the parents she had recently mourned.

They moved toward the house softly talking to each other. It was a peaceful day without a cloud in the sky. They walked up the two back steps and entered the house through the patio doors. Lillian stopped and turned around to survey the wonderful garden and inhale the scent of the fresh-cut flowers once more. When she turned back around, M&M and Doc had already entered the main house. Anticipating the cinnamon rolls and juice M&M was sure to have prepared, she stepped onto the patio and pulled the door. It was locked, or maybe just stuck. She pulled a little harder with no success. Inside the glass doors she could see them. They talked quietly and seemed not to notice her. She tapped on the glass but they did not answer.

A cool breeze now picked up outside the doors and rapidly turned to a gusting wind. The sky, clear just a minute before, was now a smoky, rapidly changing gray. Large storm clouds rolled in with urgency, and the wind became frightful. A storm was brewing. Thunder crackled in the distance but with each clap seemed to come closer. In an instant the serene morning became a raging storm. Lillian turned toward the sky. A huge bolt of lightning split the blackened clouds. That one was much closer. She decided to run for cover under the small gazebo Doc had built years earlier. As she turned to run, a brilliant flash of light struck her with tremendous force. She was knocked to the ground unable to move. The searing pain of the strike left her paralyzed. The ground shook beneath her. Her body shook with the earthquake, undulating rhythmically.

Lillian was vaguely aware that another bolt of lightning had struck, causing every nerve in her body to cry out in agony. She tried to scream but there was no sound. As she lay motionless in blistering pain, she heard a voice far in the distance say, "We got a pulse."

Acknowledgments

In the preparation and the development of this story, I would first like to thank my lovely wife, Pamela, who allowed me to disappear for hours at a time on Saturdays during the height of the pandemic. She was unaware that I was writing a novel but trusted that I was doing something constructive. When the first manuscript was completed she was the first to read it. She read it in one sitting, starting one evening and not finishing until early the next morning. I was encouraged that she found it to be compelling. I am sure she was able to recognize a number of traits developed in the beloved Marnie that were taken from my experiences of dating and our marriage. Thank you for letting me borrow those times.

Once the waters were tested with Pamela, whom I trusted implicitly to tell me the truth, I enlisted a focus group of my own family and friends to give me their feedback. My sisters, Annette Yancy and Dr. Saundra McGuire, were happy to give me their thoughts, as were my daughters and son, Shawn, Erikka and Damion. Knowing that my adopted "nieces" are avid readers, copies were given to Maya and Mychael Favors, and their Mother Tia Cavanaugh-Goggans for opinions as well. In addition, I was able to persuade my office manager Devin Wirkkala-Thompkins to read it.

Needing some outside opinions, I enlisted the help of two of my close friends and co-workers, Pat Richards, Vice President of Medical Management at a prestigious insurance company, and Robert Baker, M.D., one of the smartest and most widely read pediatricians I have ever met. Both provided considerable input for me, and their comments were definitely taken to heart.

As an independent self-employed pediatrician, the pandemic took its toll. But thanks to my sister, Dr. Saundra Yancy McGuire, an extraordinary educator, international lecturer, and author of numerous books related to chemistry and learning methods, I was able to secure the early financing. She graciously paid for the editing and also the marvelous book design by Kathleen Dyson. In addition to the financing, Saundra provided me with the absolute best editor I could have ever imagined. My, niece, Stephanie McGuire, a published author in her own right, took an incredible amount of time, energy, and sweat and laced together my sentence fragments and interrupted thoughts. She did a remarkable job in the editing process for which I am eternally grateful. Connecting with her after many years was a delightful experience, as she was able to craftily tell me what would not work in the text without hurting my feelings! It is certainly my hope that we can work together on the next project, be it fiction or non-fiction.

I would also like to acknowledge my older brother, Bob Yancy, who was an inspiration to me growing up, even though I was definitely the proverbial irritating little brother. His interest in science and his writing skills inspired me. Some of the scenes in the story concerning childhood adventures were extrapolated from some of the fun we had.

Although they will never read this work, I would like to thank my mother and father, Robert E. Yancy, Jr. and Delsie Melba Moore Yancy, whose love of education, their children, and each other inspired the affections depicted in *Cottonmouth*.

I would not consider closing without thanking all of the doctors, nurses, unit secretaries, respiratory therapists, housekeeping specialists, transportation workers, and staff of each hospital on the front lines of this incredible battle against such a deadly enemy during this pandemic. Their tireless work has saved countless lives.

In addition to them, I must also thank the grocery workers, bus drivers, sanitation workers, meat packers, schoolteachers, and every single laborer that has fought to keep us safe, fed, and clothed, and our children educated. Each is a hero in their own way.

This fictional account was written partially to underscore that each pandemic death is not just a number on a curve or a plot on a graph. Each person who has succumbed to this virus and each who is now suffering its often-debilitating effects is someone's family member or loved one. Each has an individual story to tell. Some will lament the vacations that can never again be taken with those who have passed away. Others will be haunted by a half-empty container of their beloved's favorite beverage in the refrigerator. Each of the victims takes with them quiet daily rituals and little inside jokes never to be shared again. Every life was and is interconnected in loving networks uniquely impacted by the devastating nature of the pandemic.

I must also take the time to acknowledge the sacrifices of our children. They are often the unseen victims. Though they have not suffered as much illness or death, the emotional toll on them has been and continues to be staggering. The isolation, the loss of friends, and often the actual loss of grandparents, parents, and loved ones has left them shaken in many ways. I pray that their recovery will be swift and complete once we are able to return to some form of normal.

In reading this narrative, it is my hope that you have felt the intimate pain of each of the characters. And I also hope that awareness of others' suffering brings all of us a sense of urgency to express our feelings to those we love. My prayer is that we will find the strength to conquer the next pandemic, or whatever world crisis that may befall us, with thinking and actions that benefit all. With those actions of compassion and concern we will truly become, as ordained by God, our brother's and our sister's keeper.

Eric A. Yancy, M.D.